NIGHTMARE ISLAND

SHAKIRAH BOURNE

NIGHTMARE ISLAND

SCHOLASTIC PRESS / NEW YORK

All rights reserved. Published by Scholastic Press, an imprint of Scholastic Inc., *Publishers since 1920*. SCHOLASTIC, SCHOLASTIC PRESS, and associated logos are trademarks and/or registered trademarks of Scholastic Inc.

The publisher does not have any control over and does not assume any responsibility for author or third-party websites or their content.

Library of Congress Cataloging-in-Publication Data available

ISBN 978-1-338-78357-5

10 9 8 7 6 5 4 3 2 1   23 24 25 26 27

Printed in Italy 183
First edition, June 2023

Book design by Omou Barry

*To the ancestors whose names
we never knew, but whose faces
we see in the mirror*

ESTABLISHING SHOT

This story may remind you of a wacky old horror film. Faceless children with backward feet, a deadly forest, and mutant rabbits? All that's missing is Frankenstein cackling in the background.

But everything you're about to read is true, give or take a few details because, after all, I am a storyteller. This is my story, but it's possibly yours too, if your parents ever visited a mysterious Caribbean island and returned with a perfect baby.

However, there's one thing you and I probably don't have in common. It's a secret I've never shared with a living soul.

I can hear everyone's unique soundtrack.

No one else knows this, but people have scores—like the background music you'd hear in a movie. For example, if I suddenly hear the sound of slow raindrops on dry leaves, I know my mum is nearby. Dad's music is similar, only his drops of rain gently drum on empty pavement. She's the pitter and he's the patter. Maybe that's why they get along so well.

My brother's music is a bit more complicated, but you'll soon understand why. Sometimes I can't hear it, and that silence scares me more than anything in the world.

TAKE 1—WHAT'S BEHIND THE DOOR?

For as long as I can remember, I've had the same nightmare.

It opens in a blinding-white room with nothing but silence. No birds, no crickets, no breeze.

It's the sort of atmosphere my parents love so much, they named me Serenity.

A team of doctors rush into the lobby with my heavily pregnant mother on a gurney. You may have seen a chaotic scene like this on one of those medical TV shows, but in my nightmare someone has muted the sound.

My mother grimaces and clutches her belly. But even in pain, she checks to make sure her black, straightened hair is still in place.

Then the chaos arrives. Enter six-year-old me, in my pajamas, screeching and twisting in my father's arms, and grabbing at his perfectly identical locs. He puts me down on a hard, gray couch.

A shadowed person appears above me. Their blurry face twists in shades of black, looking at me with such disgust my scream becomes a choking gurgle in my throat.

And then I'm alone.

My throat is raw but I don't stop bawling. Not until a silver butterfly appears out of nowhere and flutters onto my wet cheek.

Its wings tremble as it drinks my tears. I reach for the butterfly, but it moves away like a beam of light.

I follow the butterfly down an empty tunnel while whistling my favorite tune, "The Ants Go Marching." The butterfly floats to the floor and slips underneath a metal door with a NO ENTRY sign.

A red dot blinks twice on a shiny black panel and then I hear two quiet beeps, like a bird's chirp. The door opens with a soft hiss, and the whistle dies on my lips as I take in the sight in front of me.

And then everything fades to black . . .

I wake up covered in cold sweat. My brain screams for me to relax. *It's just a nightmare,* it chants. I feel like I'm about to throw up, so I reach for the metal bowl under my bed. Once, after the nightmare, I got dizzy on my way to the bathroom and hit my head on the bed frame, so I keep the bowl there for emergencies.

Luckily the nausea passes and the sweet potato pie I had for dinner stays in my belly. I'm never able to get back to sleep after the nightmare, so there's only one thing to do.

Create a monster.

I turn on the light and reach for my sketch pad on the dresser.

I once watched a kung fu movie where the master told his student they had to face their fear because "avoiding fear increases the fear itself." That made sense to me.

But how can I confront my fear if I have no idea what I am afraid of? I need to see the face of the monster that haunts me. I've watched every horror movie about blood-sucking vampires, flesh-eating zombies, haunted houses, you name it, but none of them have ever made my heart leap out of my chest like it does in my nightmare.

So I decided to create my own monsters, and now I'm obsessed with making the scariest horror movie of all time.

I want to know what's behind that door . . .

TAKE 2—AAANNND ACTION

That evening, I sit on the couch with my little brother, Peace, trying to ignore a headache. We're brainstorming the monster for my new film—stop-motion style.

There are a bunch of paper actors scattered around the living room, inspired by the people in my house right now. The paper mum is hosting a moonlight yoga session. The paper dad sits at his desk and stares at the wall. That's how he writes. Finally, a paper brother and sister stand in front of a cardboard door.

"I've got it!" I flip the page on my sketch pad.

"Please, Ren, they'll hear you." Peace stretches his neck out toward the garden. Behind the glass doors, fluorescent glow sticks float in the darkness like lightsabers.

Peace's soft voice always sounds like a sigh. It complements his music, which, for now, sounds like gentle brushstrokes on canvas. Meanwhile twelve years of "Hush, Serenity" and "Please lower your voice" still haven't softened my naturally high-pitched tone.

"Here's the story." I try to maintain my practiced low voice. "A man got stung by a radioactive killer bee and turns into a half-man, half-bee creature. We can call this film"—I pause for dramatic effect—*"Buzz Kill."*

Peace's expression doesn't change, but his brushstroke music becomes more intense—he is inspired. He ducks behind the antique mahogany couch with a piece of paper to work his magic.

When he's in this mood, it's like looking into a mirror. We have similar features: dark brown skin, oval-shaped brown eyes, and full lips. But my thick hair defeats the strongest hair gels, and a few marks on my skin pay tribute to film-related accidents.

I close my eyes and hum a background score for a potential murder scene. My creative process always begins with the music; I already know the bee-man will have a slow, empty heartbeat over the hum of angry bees.

Minutes later, Peace drops a grotesque paper figure behind the cardboard door, and I have to swallow my cry of delight. It has yellow-spotted skin and pointy wings protruding from its hunchback. Peace has even made the two glassy eyes glisten with nail polish.

I shut my eyes again and imagine the bee-man shooting toxic acid from its stinger. But my heart doesn't skip a beat. No racing pulse, nothing.

The bee-man isn't as scary as the monster in my

nightmare. There's still no way for me to face my fears. I sigh but then put on a happy face to hide my disappointment from Peace.

"Ace, the bee-man looks fantabulosooome!" I sing the last word, thrust my palms out in the air, and wiggle my fingers. That's the rule. You can't say "fantabulosome" without doing the dance. "It could be perfect for the film festival in September."

Peace gives his signature faint smile, the one that seems like an accident. He should know that isn't good enough for me.

"How did you do, Ace? Eh?" I egg him on, urging him to break the golden rule.

Peace checks the garden again and then repeats, "Fantabulosome!" in a voice that anyone else would use if they were talking to themselves, but that's the loudest I've ever gotten him to go. Peace does the dance and then covers his mouth and giggles.

I glance at my camera equipment in the corner. "How about a few test shots?" I suggest. "We still have twenty minutes before Mum's class is over."

Peace nods and then extends the bee-man's wings so it seems even more menacing.

You won't believe I once hated this perfect little brother who won all my parents' affection. Baby Peace didn't cry once; he yawned when he needed a diaper change. I swear, three-year-old Peace's tummy didn't even make a sound when he was hungry.

But four-year-old Peace found his way to my room one day when I was cutting out paper spiders, grabbed a crayon, and started to color perfectly within the lines. That's the first time I heard his brushstroke music. And how could I continue to dislike someone whose face lit up in delight when I showed him my stop-motion film with hairy spiders crawling along Mum's toothbrush?

Now he's the perfect production assistant.

I grab a tripod, forgetting that the camera light on top isn't attached. It flies across the living room and lands on the tiles with a loud crash, before bouncing over a tangle of cords.

At least ninety decibels.

Peace winces and covers his ears, and I squeeze the tripod, hoping and praying for a miracle. The basement studio is soundproof and maybe the thick wooden doors—

"Serenity." A sharp voice whisper-hisses from the garden.

Peace scolds me with his eyes. I drop my shoulders and head to my mother. As I pass some scented trash bags, I fish out the magazine I had earlier stuffed into a bin under the wooden shutter window.

My parents bought this old plantation house last year when Dad started tracing our family tree and discovered one of our ancestors worked here. The house is far away from the

8

main road, so there are never any traffic noises, and tonight is one of those nights when the wind has gone on vacation and taken the crickets with it.

I hum to break the quiet as I trudge toward the glow sticks.

The women stand on yoga mats with their hands clasped and one of their feet against their thighs. They sound at ease: a dripping tap, a blackbird chirping, a shak-shak tree rattling in the wind, different types of bells, and a strange purring—the lady in the white headband is going to leave a huge tip.

Mum glides over to me, her hands still clasped. Today her raindrops are scattered, falling in different patterns. She's anxious, probably because it's her first moonlight yoga class and she wants to make a good impression.

"Serenity Noah, I told you to be quiet. You almost put our cellular energy out of alignment." Mum's voice is as soft and slow as a hymn.

"Sorry, Mum, I was trying to shoot a new documentary about stars." *And not monsters.*

I hold up the *National Geographic* magazine that's been conveniently showing up in my room, no matter how many times I toss it away. I immediately know I've said the right thing. Mum's raindrops resume their gentle pitter.

"Oh!" Mum beams at the cluster of stars on the cover. "Well, just keep it down, okay?"

I nod and hurry away before she notices the tea bag stuck to the back of the magazine. I avoid the creaky spots marked

9

with caution tape on the wooden stairs and make sure I don't accidentally slam the door.

My parents are allergic to noise. I've never heard them make any sound over fifty decibels; they break out in hives at anything louder than a washing machine.

Noise drives them mad and I need it to remain sane. It's a mystery we're related.

I give Peace a triumphant smile when I get back to the living room. He's added some more paper victims to the scene, with some brilliant red slashes across their chests.

Before hitting record, I notice the blinking battery light and scurry over to a wall socket.

"Aaannnd action." I press on my remote camera trigger and plug in the camera charger at the same time.

There is a short sizzle, a loud pop, and the entire living room goes dark.

And then Peace starts to scream.

TAKE 3—BUZZ KILL

In the year 2000, a woman set the world record for the loudest scream when her earsplitting cry reached 129 decibels—as loud as a jackhammer, and only a few decibels lower than a jet taking off. If the *Guinness World Records* judges had been at my house tonight with the sound level meter, Peace would have broken that record.

When did he learn to scream like this?

I race toward his cries and bang straight into the coffee table. Suddenly there are fireworks in the darkness as I clutch my knee and drop to the floor. Then another crash, this time from the ceramic vase that rolled off the table.

"Leave me alone!" Peace shrieks in pure terror.

There is a lot of music coming toward us. A blackbird squawking. Bells knocking together. But above them all, a double rainstorm. I block out everything and focus on Peace, but I can't hear his brushstrokes.

He's screaming but his music has gone silent again. I pat

the ground ahead, trying to avoid the broken ceramic pieces. "I'm coming, Ace!"

Immediately the air is filled with a hush. It's pitch-black but I can feel my parents' disapproving expressions. There's a loud surge, about seventy decibels, and then the lights in the house flicker on.

Imagine yourself at the dentist. Picture a needle the size of an ice pick, moving closer and closer to your gums. Freeze! Now look at your reflection in the metal basin. See your grimace as your eyes fill with worry, waiting for the inevitable pain? That's how my parents have looked at me for as long as I can remember.

But they've never looked at Peace that way . . . until now.

He's pressed against a bookcase, eyes wide open and staring at nothing, with snot running down his chin. His hands are tight over his ears and he pants in ragged breaths.

I've never seen him so scared.

I crawl around the ceramic pieces and touch his leg. Peace's eyes roll to the back of his head, and his scream reaches a whole new octave until his voice cracks from the effort. My parents flinch and cover their ears and then rush toward us.

"Ace, it's me!" I cry, but my voice doesn't penetrate his scream.

I manage to dodge his kick to my face, and he doesn't stop kicking. Several items in the living room endure his wrath: the couch, the coffee table, the TV stand with Dad's collection of encyclopedias. Luckily Dad catches him before he attacks the glass cabinets, but Peace slips out of his grip.

He squeezes under a chair and curls into a tight ball, making soft mewling noises, and trembles so hard the chair rattles on the polished wood.

I move over to the chair, but I don't touch him again in case it triggers another outburst.

Mum bends down next to me, flooding my nostrils with the smell of shea butter and orange oil. "It's all right, sugar dumpling."

Peace opens his eyes and reaches for Mum. Still shaking, he buries his face in her chest, and his mewling noises turn into sniffles as she rains small puckered kisses on top of his head.

Then she notices the bee-man and plucks it from the couch with disgust. "Serenity Noah, you're scaring your brother with these horror movies!"

I want to protest, but I can't stop staring at Peace trembling in my mother's arms. It's as if he saw what was behind that door in my nightmare. No way the bee-man could have caused this reaction.

Mum takes in the paper people on the sofa, with their various missing arms and legs and bloody slashes on their chests, and the very expensive, very broken vase. But the real horror comes when her gaze lands on the open-mouthed yoga women by the door.

"Everything's fine, everything's fine, the kids were just playing around," she reassures them, while knocking the paper victims out of sight. "That's it for today. Did I mention this first class is free if you leave a positive review?"

Dad leads the women away while promising signed copies of his book.

Mum keeps her frozen smile in place until she's sure everyone is gone, and then she tilts her head and exhales her frustration.

"Why are you like this, child?" Mum's voice is quiet but the words cut deep.

I take a deep breath, preparing to use what my parents call my "inside voice." "I'm sorry, I was just trying to get a good shot."

Dad sighs and then gets a broom and dustpan to sweep up the broken vase.

"I'm tired of these morbid movies that you never finish. Why are there so many ugly thoughts in your beautiful head?" Mum complains.

For the hundredth time, I wonder if I should confess about my nightmares, but I worry they'd blame horror movies and ban me from watching them. So instead I just shrug.

"Now they're affecting your brother. I don't want him involved in these creepy films anymore."

"But, Mum—"

Peace lifts his head. "I'm not afraid of the bee-man. There was—there was something in the dark."

"A bloody ghost with sharp teeth?" The question slips out before I can stop it.

Dad gives me his standard look of bewilderment, like I'm a puzzle with a missing piece.

"You sure your sister didn't scare you?" Mum asks. "You've never been afraid of the dark before."

"You can tell us," Dad prods in a gentle voice.

Peace bites his lip and, to my relief, shakes his head.

"The shadows in the dark." He makes a soft whimpering noise. "They called my name. They want to take me away."

His words send a shiver through me. My parents do that thing where they stare at each other and have a whole conversation in their heads. Then Mum taps her fingertips together and chants a relaxation mantra under her breath.

Dad immediately goes into fix-it mode. "Okay, Naamah, they were raving about the class, so no real harm done. And you, buddy, how 'bout you sleep with us tonight?" He lifts Peace from Mum's lap and then gestures around with his chin. "Serenity, put away your toys," he says, as if I'm two instead of twelve. I bite my tongue and start to clear the film set.

Mum starts to follow them upstairs but then turns. "Serenity, no more horror films. And I don't want you talking to Peace about monsters either. It's time you make other kinds of movies or none at all."

My body starts to shake with anger, and I unintentionally crush the bee-man in my fist. "You can't be serious."

She crosses her arms. "You're scaring your brother with these movies. You're scaring *me*, for heaven's sake."

I sink down onto the couch. Mum doesn't realize she's taking away my only weapon against my nightmares. You'd think I'm lucky to have creative parents, but they've never even bothered to look at any of my footage. They've wanted a reason to stop me from making these films, and now they finally have one.

I rush to my room and flop face-first onto my pillow. I reach for my iPod and headphones on the nightstand and exhale when the music caresses my eardrums; my spouge remix of "The Ants Go Marching" never fails to relax me.

I fell in love with the musical style when Dad first introduced me to its creator, Jackie Opel. It's really fun—try chanting the words *a chicken* and you'll hear the spouge rhythm in your head. Add some guitar strums, horns, or shake a cowbell, and you have yourself a funky tune with a cool country-and-western feel.

Sadly all music-history classes came to an end when I raced through the house scream-singing "a chicken" at the top of my lungs. One day, when I'm home alone, I'll sing "a chicken" as loud as I want.

I twirl the crushed bee-man in my hands. Peace's shadows

have no name, no shape, and no backstory, but they are already way scarier than this film. They would be great monsters in a horror movie, and now I may never get a chance to make it.

I toss the bee-man into the trash.

If I'm scaring Mum now, I can't imagine her reaction if I told her about my nightmares. My parents will never understand why making horror films is so important to me. It's the best way to face my fears and take the power away from my nightmare. One day, I'll open that metal door and laugh at the monster inside.

I don't care what Mum says. I won't give up until I make a movie terrifying enough to scare my nightmares away.

TAKE 4—TWO'S A CROWD

It's been a week and Peace is still so scared of the shadows, he refuses to sleep alone.

My parents tried everything: keeping the light on, limited screen time, sneaking out after he'd fallen asleep, a night-light, glow-in-the-dark stars, meditation, you name it, but nothing worked.

Peace spends the whole night tossing, turning, and kicking. Dad suggested they take him to some doctor, but Mum balked at the idea.

Soon my parents couldn't hide the dark circles around their eyes. Mum canceled her yoga sessions and Dad complained he was too tired to write.

Every morning at breakfast, I have to ignore my parents' hostile glances from across the table. My brother's the one keeping them up at night, yet they found a way to blame me and not perfect Peace.

Still I can't help but wonder if this new fear of the dark

really is my fault. I *have* spent the last few years creating all sorts of monsters with him. I felt guilty enough to offer to let Peace sleep with me last night. It was a big mistake. I put up with Peace's kicks for a few hours, but then had to escort him back to my parents' room around two a.m.

That's why I can't understand how Mum's now zipping about the kitchen, looking as fresh as a cover model for a magazine shoot, her loose floral dress dancing in the air around her. On the dining room table are platters of pumpkin fritters, fish cakes, and spinach fries.

Mum notices me on the stairs and gives a brilliant smile— the first smile she's given me in a week. "Serenity, my darling, I was just coming to get you."

I glance around to make sure there's no other "Serenity, my darling" behind me.

When I face her again, the smell of fried flour whacks me in the face. Not buckwheat, spelt, or any other healthy flour that's "just as good as the real thing." It's not even my birthday. Or Peace's. His is next Friday, and I saved up to give him a special surprise.

I'm savoring a moist piece of salted cod when Dad and Peace join me at the table.

Peace still has no music; he's quieter than a feather in the wind. He's the only person I've met whose music disappears. It's extra distressing because he's my favorite person in the world, and I can't hear him. He doesn't seem alive.

"Ace, it's the real stuff," I whisper, trying to revive my Peace. "Actual flour."

"I'm not hungry," he says, pushing a pumpkin fritter around on his plate.

Mum places a large bowl of sliced mangoes on the table, but when she puts a whole Julie mango in front of me, I stop eating and narrow my eyes with suspicion.

She always complains when I insist on eating mangoes the way the universe intended—not sliced and diced in perfect cubes, but slurping the messy, juicy flesh right from the skin. Why are they trying to butter me up?

"Okay, just tell me," I ask, eating two fritters at once. "What's going on?"

"We can talk after breakfast," Dad replies, exchanging a look with Mum. "And take your time. Choking is the fourth leading cause of unintentional deaths."

He brushes some crumbs off his white dashiki shirt. He has a closet full of those cotton shirts since he changed his name from Peter to Adisa five years ago. It means "the one who makes his meaning clear," and I can't think of a name that suits him more. All the shirts look identical to me, but he seems to know the difference.

I swallow my fritters and show him my empty mouth. "I shouldn't be punished for losing a wrestling match with Peace, but let's just get it over with. No TV? No internet?"

"Darling, keep your voice down, everything's fine," Mum says, forcing another smile.

"What sort of punishment starts with a meal like this?" Dad pulls his hair from his face in one swift movement and ties it together with one of the locs. A natural hair tie.

I cock my head, still suspicious. "A last meal. And you know certain monsters like to fatten up their victims before eating them."

"Well, we're your parents, not monsters," Mum says, cutting into her fritter with a knife and fork. Then she squares her shoulders. "So as you know, Peace has been really stressed lately. We've decided to take him on a little vacation for his birthday next week—you know, a change of scenery may help."

I perk up in my seat. "Oooooh, where're we going? Bermuda? Grenada? Oh, let's do California!" My parents both wince when my voice gets extra squeaky.

I try to control my excitement and continue with my inside voice. "We can tour Universal Studios. What's more relaxing than the movie sets for *Psycho* and *Jaws* . . . and *How the Grinch Stole Christmas*," I add, after seeing the expression on Mum's face.

Mum clears her throat and puts down her utensils. "So, Serenity, we're thinking this time, it'll be just us and Peace. You can stay with Gran; you know she's always happy to see you."

"Very funny," I reply with a snort. "So where're we going?" My parents stare at me until it sinks in that it's not a joke. They're really planning on leaving me behind.

"You can't do this!" I roar, not caring about the decibels. Mum and Dad flinch again, but this time they don't scold me.

"Darling, darling, deep breaths," Mum says, and then exhales. "Listen, it's a silent retreat and you would hate it. You can't even make it through thirty minutes of family meditation, much less an entire week on Duppy Island."

"Duppy?! You're going to an island named after an evil spirit without me?" I yelp.

I know all about duppies thanks to Gran, who was quite horrified when she found out we were moving into a plantation house, or as she calls it, a "death house." Many enslaved people died here, and Dad believes there are several unmarked graves around the property. Gran thinks the spirits are angry they weren't buried properly and have turned into duppies—malicious spirits that haunt people at night. She made us do libations: sprinkling alcohol on the grounds to pacify the spirits and keep duppies away.

Mum refolds a napkin on the table. "Serenity, the name doesn't mean anything. It's just a space for people who want peace."

"But I don't want to miss Peace's birthday. Please," I beg.

I'll be stuck with Gran and about twenty of her nosy

neighbors, drowning in *Wheel of Fortune* marathons. I don't mind the clatter, but it's impossible to film with her six cats pouncing on my paper actors.

"Don't worry, we'll take a solo vacation with you later this year," Mum replies, her eyes begging me to understand. "We can go to Universal Studios and, you know, look at giant, bloodthirsty sharks."

"I don't *want* to go to Universal Studios without Peace. I want him there. With me. What kind of parent abandons their child?"

The air at the table changes. Mum's rain comes down a bit harder, and immediately Dad's music becomes more intense as well.

"That's enough, Serenity." Dad gives me a warning glare.

I know it's a risk to continue when Dad's using his serious voice, but I'm not ready to give up.

"Seriously, I can be quiet. Look." I fold my lips tightly, and immediately realize it's a terrible idea because I can no longer plead my case. Dad can't hide the smug look on his face.

I put in my headphones, making sure the music's not loud enough to disturb my parents, and search for Duppy Island on my phone. I've never heard of it before. I wonder why my parents would choose to go on vacation to an island with such a creepy name.

It's not often that I search for a term and only get three

hits. The first link directs me to some Caribbean mythology chat room, but the site is restricted.

The last two are illustrations of duppies—one of them is a creature with bulging eyes, whose smile takes up almost its entire face. Another is a rotting doll-like creature with bloodshot eyes and a mouth stuck in an O. She holds a doll in her hand that looks just like her, except it's smiling and there are tears flowing from its red eyes.

Footage of Duppy Island would be the *perfect* setting for my first live-action horror film . . . and I'm not allowed to go. I slump in my chair and sigh.

Mum places her hand on top of mine, and I think she's being affectionate until I realize I've been drumming the spouge beat on the table.

It's been two minutes and I've already lost the silence game. Peace pushes a half-eaten fritter away and sags in his chair.

Suddenly I understand why my parents want to take a solo vacation with Peace.

They need to take a vacation to get away from me.

TAKE 5—MARK MY WORDS

My parents stop talking as soon as I enter the living room.

I ignore their forced smiles, drop my old duffel bag next to their eco-friendly green-and-brown luggage by the door, and head back upstairs.

I haven't spoken to them since they told me I wasn't invited on their vacation. For the last few days they've been trying to get back on my good side, making my favorite foods and having movie nights with the volume ten decibels higher than normal.

If only they knew I could hear the thunder and lightning behind their fake smiles.

I step into Peace's bedroom with my hands behind my back. He's been a sullen, mopey figure, but his face brightens when I surprise him with the wrapped gift.

"Happy birthday in advance, Ace."

He carefully unwraps the paper and unveils the set of acrylic paints. He's so excited, his brushstroke music breaks through the silence.

Warm joy fills my heart. See? I can do some things right.

Peace has made enough paper monsters for me to realize he has a special gift for painting. Mum and Dad will be thrilled; it's their dream to have a "real artist" in the family. Some of my warmth chills to cold jealousy, but that's how it is with Peace. Even as I love him, I am envious at the same time.

Then, just as quickly as his music returned, it disappears.

"You don't like it?" I ask, trying to hide my disappointment. "I can exchange it for something else."

"It's not that. I just—I just wish you were coming with us," he says, flicking the hairs on a paintbrush. He's going to be gone for three weeks; we've never been apart for so long.

"Don't worry, you're going to have fun. Sitting and thinking and . . . sitting." I have no idea what people actually do at a silent retreat.

"Something just doesn't feel right," he replies, and then leans forward. "The shadows are happy," he whispers.

A tingle goes down my spine. Peace tilts the fluorescent paints to the side, fascinated by how they flow to the top of the containers.

"Let me get you some canvas so you can paint on the trip," I say, shaking off my emotions. Mum keeps a roll of it in the studio to sometimes use in her ASMR videos—recordings of her doing things like whispering into a mic or shampooing wigs.

When I get downstairs, my parents are in the kitchen,

speaking in extra-hushed tones. I duck behind the wall to read their lips; it's another skill that developed out of my fear of silence.

No one knows about this secret either.

"Adisa, I don't think we can afford this," Mum is saying.

"Maybe we can get another loan from the bank, or I can work on a new book." Dad leans against the counter and rubs his eyes.

He lowers his head to read from a paper in his hands and I can't see his lips, but when he raises his head again, I recognize the words *shadows* and *this should help*.

Normally I don't catch every single word, so there must be some mistake. We've never seemed strapped for cash, but it must have been expensive to buy the plantation house. Another buyer wanted to turn it into a tourist attraction, but Dad made a higher offer and said it was worth every penny to "reclaim our history and honor our ancestors."

I make out *catch the ferry* before Dad steps in front of Mum and hugs her.

"All for our perfect child," Mum says, loud enough so I don't have to lip-read, before burying her face in his neck.

Ouch.

That hurt.

It hurt so much.

It's one thing to know Peace is the favorite and another to have it confirmed out loud.

I sneak downstairs and slip into my parents' studio. It's way messier than usual, with Dad's books piled on his desk and on the floor, and the giant whiteboard filled with Dad's scratchy handwriting, charts, and drawings. There are dozens of photocopies of old newspapers swallowing the white walls.

At first, all of us were involved in researching the family tree. My great-grandmother was in a folk singing group, and my great-grandpa, who was a tailor, made all their outfits. And my great-great-grandmother was a cook on a sugar plantation—the one that's now our home—but Gran only knew the first name of my great-great-great-grandmother. That's when things got boring because we've had to search through thousands of records, online archives, and plantation ledgers. Most of them are incomplete or damaged, but Dad hasn't given up. "Understanding our history is the best way to understand ourselves," he says.

I search for the canvas in the chaos, still troubled by my parents' conversation. Why are they bothering with an expensive vacation if money is tight? It costs nothing to send me to Gran's house and stay at home.

I check the giant mahogany desk, hoping to find information about their trip to Duppy Island, but there's no time to sift through the tower of papers and books. The taxi will arrive soon to take me to Gran's, and then my parents and Peace to the port.

In desperation, I pull out my phone and search for Duppy Island again, but I get the same three hits. Then I realize I can access the Caribbean mythology site if I create an account. I do it quickly while keeping an eye on the door. After I log in, I scan the messages in the forum and my eyes linger on the last comment from Captain%H2O.

Duppy Island is cursed. The souls of children who died before they were baptized live in the forest. Evil faceless douens. Stay AWAY if you know what's good for you.

Faceless children? I've never heard of a concept so horrific and thrilling at the same time. I do a search for douens and my breath catches in my throat when I see the first image.

It's an illustration of a small child in a mushroom-shaped hat; it's almost large enough to hide that the creature has no eyes and nose—only a small, gaping mouth. The rest of its body is normal, except for its feet; they're twisted backward in a painful-looking way, as if someone broke its ankles.

I close my eyes, imagining a douen behind the door in my nightmare, and my heart starts to thump in my chest.

It is much scarier than the bee-man. Scarier than shadows in the dark.

This could be it.

No other monster has given me chills. I'm going to bring this creature to life on film.

A movie about an evil douen who sneaks into houses to steal children's faces. I could call it . . . *The Face Snatcher.*

The name makes my heart skip a beat.

This is it. I can feel it in my bones. I find the roll of canvas in the corner and get upstairs just when the taxi arrives.

As we drive away from the plantation, I clutch the bag with my film gear, glad I decided to still pack my camera, lenses, and tripod.

I plan to kill two birds with one stone—be with Peace on his birthday and get footage for my new horror film. A film that may be scarier than my nightmare. It's the masterpiece I've been searching for, and no good filmmaker ignores inspiration.

I'm going to Duppy Island, whether I'm invited or not.

TAKE 6—THE CAPTAIN'S TALE

There should be a movie about a girl, a brave young film-maker, being pursued by angry aunties and snarling cats. She'd manage to avoid their razor-sharp claws in the nick of time and leap into a sleek convertible just before it moved off. Make sure to use a James Bond–like score or, for a lighter atmosphere, that classic music from a Bugs Bunny chase scene.

That scenario is much more exciting than what actually happened, because it was dead easy to throw a backpack with a few clothes and my film equipment through the front window, tell my gran I was going to buy a snack from the shop down the road, and hop in a ZR taxi to follow my parents to the port.

They never let me take a ZR anywhere, and I finally understand why. The latest dancehall music blares from the speakers as the van zips around sharp corners, and the conductor hangs out the door to solicit passengers. It's not that different from a car chase scene in a movie, especially when a police jeep turns on sirens to report the speeding and the van cuts through an alley to escape.

The dock is located in the middle of the city center, surrounded by honking traffic and tourists taking selfies in the middle of the streets.

I ignore Gran's call and rush to the entrance, hoping I didn't miss the ferry.

"Young lady, I have never heard about no Duppy Island," says the security guard, who seems more interested in her phone than in providing actual security.

She sounds like the popping noises in a video game.

This doesn't make any sense, though it would explain why I couldn't find anything about the island online. But my family isn't swimming to the silent retreat, so there must be a boat somewhere. I crane my neck around, hoping to see my parents in their large noise-cancellation headphones. They wear them when they go to town so their "thoughts won't be disturbed."

I pull out my phone and ignore Gran's call again. "I wish people would stop sending me so many Candy Crush lives," I say, aiming to get the guard's attention.

The security guard swivels around in her chair. "You have extra lives?!"

After I transfer the lives, the guard suggests I speak to "the Captain" and points out a short, bearded man in a sleeveless jacket in the distance, near the souvenir stalls.

I hurry to him, and as I get closer the music of tumbling sand fills the air. "Excuse me! Captain!"

He greets me with a frown and checks his watch.

"I'd like to get to Duppy Island, and the security guard said you could help?"

"She was wrong," he replies, and walks away.

I hurry behind him, dodging tourists in Hawaiian shirts slapping on sunblock and asking for directions.

"Please, sir, I was late for my parents' ferry and now it's gone. I really don't want to miss out on the family vacation—I've been looking forward to it for weeks."

The Captain releases a bark of laughter. "That boat wouldn't have left if you were supposed to be on it. Do yourself a favor and go home."

"But—"

He disappears in a sea of tourists disembarking a cruise ship, and I'm shoved aside by taxi men haggling them for island tours.

By the time I escape the crowd, there's no sign of the Captain. I walk along the dock, listening for the Captain's tumbling sand soundtrack, but it's impossible when you're practically next to the beach.

After a few minutes, I trudge back to the bus stop along the dock, trying not to cry. I had assumed once I got to the port and onto the ferry, my parents would be forced to keep me with them. Now I'll probably be grounded for sneaking out, and who knows what punishment Gran will come up with—I bet it'll be cat related.

"Horace, check the reflector for when we get near Duppy Island," says a hoarse voice.

I whirl around in time to see the Captain hopping into a small white-and-blue ferry. He throws a large blue tarp over a stack of crates.

Standing a few feet away are a fashionably dressed man in a black tux and woman in a white ballroom gown who echo a symphony of violins.

"I can't wait to see my dear little Eloise," the woman says to the man as she boards the boat.

What I'm about to do next is a bad idea. A terrible idea. So why do I still sneak aboard and hide underneath the tarp?

Because a good filmmaker does whatever's necessary to get their shot.

Soon the port noises grow more distant and are replaced by the splash of the waves and low hum of an engine.

I'm pressed against some crates—I can't tell what's inside them, but it smells like a tower of old shoes filled with rotten eggs. And it's boiling under here. I could have tolerated the space if it weren't for the sounds of insects scuttling around under the tarp. Cockroaches? Mice? A mutant combination of the two? They scramble up and down the crates, hitting against the plastic like chattering teeth.

It takes all my willpower not to scream and lunge from

under the tarp. Instead I claw at my clothing, so the creatures know I won't go down without a fight. I need to get as far away from the port as possible, or at least far enough so the boat won't turn back if they find me. But soon the pungent smell makes me light-headed, and I have to lift the edge of the tarp with my little finger to sneak in a breath of fresh air.

An ashy foot with jagged, aged toenails nearly crushes my pinkie.

"I hate going to this place, hear, Horace?" A pair of feet as broad as tennis rackets join his. I like this Horace; his music reminds me of fish hooks clinking together and it makes for a fun, chiming melody.

"What's the problem, Cap? I thought we just dropping off and collecting cargo?"

"You don't know the story about Duppy Island?" the Captain says, twitching his toes. Then he sits down on the crate.

Something tickles my ankle. I use a washcloth to slap at the area, then curl my feet against my chest. Sweat pours from my forehead and armpits, and I want to use the washcloth to wipe it away, but what if there's a large spider clinging to the threads?

"Back in the day, during the cholera outbreak, they built a quarantine facility on that island for sick people. To send them to their death, to be honest. No cure back then—you live or you die, and most people died. But then one day, the island went radio silent. Dog bite yuh, when the rescue crew got there, the whole place empty-empty, everybody—nurses, doctors, cleaners, patients—all gone, not even a housefly. Nobody except one of the sick people, half buried in the dirt and mumbling gibberish. A young fella, probably as young as you."

"Cap, I'm forty. But that's half your age, right?"

The Captain gives him a swift kick, and Horace yelps but then laughs. I take advantage of the noise and slap at my bare arms. The bugs are drawn to my sweat, which has now soaked through my T-shirt and jeans.

"Shut up and listen, I ain't telling this again. Anyway, the crew wanted to leave him there to die, disease was so contagious, you get me? But the poor kid was crying out for his mother, so they took him back to the mainland. By the time they reach, his skin was wrinkle-up like a raisin. And gray-gray, like cement. They spread the word and searched for his mother, but only a pastor came. Took one look at him and prayed for a quick death. And the prayer worked. Boy died soon after."

The Captain's toes curl together and his music changes; his sand becomes a dune, the grains piling on top of one another instead of tumbling free.

The good part is coming. I lift the tarp a little higher to let in some more fresh air and suspense.

"The graveyards had run out of room to bury the dead, and since no one claimed the body, they put him in a crocus bag and threw him in a sandpit to burn with the other victims. You know Fin's snorkeling shack?"

"Next to Cod's fish fry? Near the beach?"

"Yep, hundreds of people got burn-up on that spot. But the boy wasn't one of them."

I almost interrupt to ask if his mother came to get him after all, and I have to bite my tongue again. It's just a story, but I would feel better knowing he wasn't just abandoned by his family.

"When they went to burn the next set of bodies, they found him intact. In. Tact. Not a mark on that gray skin. People thought his skin was too tough to burn, but when they turned him over, his whole face was gone."

I am riveted and my mouth forms an O. I didn't see that twist coming! I wish I could record this.

"They tried to burn him five more times that day. Used kerosene, oil, coal, but nothing worked. Crowds started gathering to watch them try, like it was the circus or something. It would have turned into a whole show but they never got the chance to burn him again. Next day the body was gone and a fishing boat missing. Guess where they found it?"

Horace's toes perk up. "You gotta be kidding me."

"Nope. Same place we're headed now. And there was no one on the boat either, nothing but two black, sooty

37

handprints on the paddle. After that, so many visitors to the island went missing, people say the fog swallowed them. We sent the diseased there, and the land got sick as well. And folks have to whisper so they don't wake up the dead. That's how it got the name Duppy. For the evil spirits that live there."

I'm on my way to an island where the fog eats people for breakfast. I can't imagine a more perfect setting for a horror movie.

"Sounds like hogwash to me," Horace replies, scratching his very big toe.

"Maybe it's just an old wives' tale. But the flying fish, tuna, marlin—all the fish disappear from the water around the island too. And I don't trust any place where the sea can starve you."

"True, true," Horace replies. "But what about the demon children that live in the forest?"

There is an eerie silence; even the vermin under the tarp seem to have abandoned ship. I perk up against the crate. The Captain's tumbling sand now sounds like it's falling off a cliff.

He is afraid.

"I don't know what you talkin' about," the Captain finally responds.

"But—"

"I say I don't know!" he hisses. "Now go and check the

reflector!" Horace walks away, mumbling about old men drinking too much seawater.

I lean against the crate again, thoughts racing through my brain. Horace must have been referring to douens, and it's clear the Captain lied to avoid the subject. But why would a tough sea captain be so freaked out by faceless children he can't even talk about them? Doesn't he know it's all folklore and not real?

Unless . . .

My stomach does a little flip. I almost chew on my fingernail but then remember it's dirty with crate grime. For a second, I wonder if it was a mistake to sneak to Duppy Island but then push the thought away. My parents wouldn't take Peace to a place that's dangerous. Douens are definitely not real. The Captain's fear is a good sign that my film will truly be the scariest horror movie of all time.

As time passes, I drift off to sleep, thinking about new scenes for my *Face Snatcher* movie and my family's shocked expressions when I surprise them on Duppy Island.

TAKE 7—DUPPY ISLAND

The ugliest, most discordant music wakes me up.

It reminds me of the hopeless cry of a toddler who's lost their parents, or maybe parents who've lost a toddler—whichever is worse.

The sound is so loud it overpowers everyone; I can't even hear if the Captain and the rest of the crew are nearby, so I take a chance and push my head out from the tarp.

Everything is gray, like the sun suddenly decided to take a nap and pulled the covers over its rays. Dark clouds hover above giant trees, like a halo. Better get a sweeping drone aerial shot, else it'll just look like giant heads of steaming broccoli on a plate.

The island seems moody, as if it's upset that I'm here. I rub my hands over the goose bumps on my arms. After being trapped under the hot tarp, the chill stings my sweaty skin, making me tremble, though it's almost midday.

I check my phone, but there's no signal. What now? I have to get off the boat and find the silent retreat. I need a plan, but it's so hard to concentrate with that awful crying.

I jump when someone pulls a crate along the deck and duck back under the tarp.

"Horace, quiet! But move fast so we can get out of here," the Captain hisses in a low voice.

I nearly scream when they lift away the tarp, but instead I bite my tongue and scurry around the opposite side of the crates. If they remove all the crates from the boat, I'll have nowhere left to hide.

I take a peek out to shore from the opposite side of the boat and gasp.

There's an alien aircraft, or something close to one, on a wooden jetty. It looks like a sleek blimp, if there is such a thing. There's no branding, no logo, just a perfect white oval that looks like an egg balanced on top of a helicopter. I snap a quick picture with my phone and hope that I live long enough to collect the National Geographic photo award.

The fancy couple stands a short distance away from the spaceship. They're talking to a tall, bald man in a white jacket, whose smooth brown head gleams brighter than a newly minted coin. Someone, most likely Horace, drops a crate. The man in the white jacket whirls around and the awful cry intensifies.

It's his music! This is the first time I've ever disliked anyone at first sound.

He's partially blocked, and I'm glad because I don't want

to see the face of someone with such a terrible soundtrack. I hope I never run into him again.

Suddenly a little girl who reminds me of Peace steps out from behind her mother. It's dear little Eloise. She wears a knee-length flare dress, and looks like an old Barbie doll I used to play with before it got trapped under a hot stove and its head refused to stay on.

Eloise turns toward the boat and our eyes meet. It's too late to move. I expect her to blow my cover, but she gives me a hesitant smile that is eerily similar to Peace's "I'm being polite" face.

I put a finger on my lips to tell her to remain quiet and she nods, then I duck out of sight.

Think, think—how am I going to get out of this? I would hate to make it all this way only for the Captain to carry me right back to the port.

I take another peek in time to see Eloise about to step onto the boat. She doesn't notice a rusty broken nail protruding from the rotting wood of the jetty. Before I can whisper a warning, Eloise presses her small, pale hand down on the nail, and it disappears into her flesh. Her body stiffens and her mouth twists in agony.

I brace myself for the inevitable wail, but it never comes.

"What's the matter, Eloise? Get in the boat," her dad says, still unaware of the accident.

"Give her a minute to say goodbye. You're going to miss coming to the island, aren't you, Eloise?"

Eloise bows her head and nods to her parents. She looks down at her hand with a worried expression, and then right at me. She takes a deep breath and yanks her hand from the rusty nail.

I groan, my stomach queasy as I imagine her distress. I really hope the Captain has a first aid kit; the girl must be in shock. The tears and screams are going to come any minute.

Pain builds in her eyes, and without a word, she hides her wounded hand in her pocket. She pulls herself onto the boat with her uninjured hand, leaving me staring at the trail of blood rolling down the wood.

I can't believe she'd rather rip away the flesh from her hand than disobey her mother. And I thought Peace was eager to please . . .

Then I spot a small set of stairs, which must lead onto the front deck. I check to make sure everyone is still distracted on the jetty and then race up the stairs.

I press against the outside of the cockpit. The only thing I can do is wait for everyone to leave the jetty, then jump off the boat and swim for it. Hopefully I'll find someone at a gas station or restaurant who can give directions to the silent retreat.

A minute later, there's a sound similar to a cat's purr. The spaceship has taken flight. It rises into the air, and the clouds twist together, as if a tornado is about to form.

Then the boat starts its engine.

It's now or never. I stuff my phone into my backpack, grateful it's waterproof, and climb over the stern.

"Stop!" the Captain yelps behind me. I'm so startled I lose my balance on the edge. My arms flail in the air, but a strong grip stops my epic belly flop into the sea. There's a small splash below as a plastic heavy-duty flashlight falls into the water.

Busted.

The Captain clutches on to me like I'm a freshly caught fish desperate to hop back into the ocean.

"You trying to dead?" he rasps. A glistening piece of slime crawls over the flashlight and pulls it underwater.

"Giant jellyfish," the Captain says, scowling at my shocked face. "Deadly poisonous. They sting first and ask questions later. They're almost invisible now, but it's like aurora borealis at night."

I shudder at the thought of coming so close to death while the Captain pulls me to the back of the ship.

The fancy couple and a tall, lanky man who I assume is Horace gape at me in surprise. I'm sure I don't look my best with my red T-shirt and jeans covered in sweat and crate grime.

The Captain and Horace argue about what to do with me

because they're already behind schedule, but access to land is strictly forbidden. I feel like a package sent to the wrong address that's not worth the return postage. If he doesn't buy my lie and takes me back to the mainland, I will have gone through all this trouble for nothing.

"Horace, keep an eye on her," he says, frowning and checking his watch again. "I'm going to radio this *retreat*. You said your parents are the Noahs?"

The little bit of hope dies inside me. I bet my parents will tell them to carry me back to the port.

Before he goes into the cockpit, the Captain lowers his head to my ear. "You're lucky I caught you. This place doesn't like uninvited guests."

The warning sends a tingle down my back. Suddenly it seems even colder outside.

There's an awkward silence as everyone waits for the Captain to return with the final verdict.

Eloise's mother takes in my messy hair and disheveled clothes and purses her lips in displeasure. I fidget under her scrutiny.

"Dr. Whisper will fix you up, good and proper," she says with a humph.

What doctor is she talking about? And it's her daughter who needs medical attention. I glance at Eloise; her face is so still she might as well not have one. I'm even more disturbed that she reminds me of Peace.

That's when I make a decision. Horace is distracted securing the remaining crates with some rope, and Eloise's dad shuffles around the deck with his phone in the air, trying to get a signal.

No one notices when I inch toward the jetty. Except Eloise. Her eyes widen and the blood seems to drain from her already pale face.

She mouths something to me.

Stay away from the bushes.

If she thinks a few trees and shrubs will stop me, she's got another thing coming. I take another step and Eloise glances up at her mother and then at me. She's going to rat me out!

I hop onto the jetty and dash toward a pebbly beach that's as big as our living room.

"Wait!" Horace cries.

I check to see if he's coming after me, but the only movement comes from Eloise. She waves goodbye to me with the bloody hand and a disturbing smile on her face.

It's only while I'm crashing through the bushes that I realize why Eloise reminds me so much of Peace.

She doesn't have any music either.

TAKE 8—THE SILVER BUTTERFLY

What do you do when you're lost in the woods? If you're a filmmaker like me, you take advantage of the situation, whip out your camera, and pretend you're in a found-footage horror film.

The thick bushes don't move in the slight wind, as if glued to one another. I hum as I venture hopefully toward civilization. My phone has to pick up some Wi-Fi signal eventually so I can find the retreat. The air becomes foggier and the gray mist clings to the trees, making them look like they're wrapped in spiderweb.

I'm tempted to put in my headphones to calm my nerves, but I need to hear the distant sounds of cars or buses. And people's music. I want to know if anyone is sneaking up behind me.

It's eerily quiet. The last time I walked through a forest, the sound of the wind through the trees was as loud as a waterfall crashing onto rocks, but Duppy Island is like distant white noise, as if I have on my parents' noise-cancellation headphones.

Where is the wildlife? There are no tweeting birds or chirping crickets. No sign of lizards, spiders, not even a rat—though I'm mighty grateful for that. After an hour, the ball of fear I've been suppressing threatens to burst, but I force myself to stay calm.

I've researched survival tips for my various "lost in the woods" movies, and the first tip is do not panic. Keeping a positive mental attitude helps to combat stress and helps you to make better, safer decisions.

I turn by two moss-covered trees that seem to embrace each other, and as I make a mental note of the landmark, the sound of the forest changes. From distant white noise to the echo of a drum. I listen closely and pivot in a circle until I determine the noise is coming from an area where the trees twist and grow close to one another.

It's worth checking out, since the trees seem more alive there than anywhere else. I move toward the area, hoping to see a hotel with infinity pool balconies in the distance, and start to whistle my favorite "The Ants Go Marching" tune to show my mind I'm in good spirits. Maybe a bird will answer.

But something else responds.

With a giggle.

I stop whistling and whirl around, but no one's there. The wind must be playing tricks with me.

"Hello?" I call to the trees. No answer, but behind me there's a slight rustling in a small bush with a handful of tiny white flowers.

I hear more chords in the air by the twisty trees, and when I turn to go toward them again, the bush with the flowers starts to serenade me.

The *hurrah* note in "The Ants Go Marching" whistles from the leaves. And there's guitar music. It sounds like a welcome-home hug after a long trip.

I get the strange urge to go closer to the bush and touch the flowers. I don't understand why. Dad's the one who cares about different plants and their origins and medicinal uses. I've never thought of bushes as more than a backdrop for my frame, but my yearning is so strong it feels like a rope tied to my wrist, pulling me closer and closer to the leaves.

When I'm near enough to touch the bush with my fingertips, Eloise's warning seems to whisper through the trees: *Stay away from the bushes.*

I take a hesitant step back.

"Is anyone there?" I call again. Nothing. Not even the whistle.

But I know I didn't imagine it. Maybe the clouds around the island are somehow delaying echoes?

Then something rises from the bush.

A silver butterfly.

My lips begin to tremble and I try to scream, but no sound comes from my throat. My brain screams for me instead, and suddenly I'm back in the tunnel in my nightmare, standing in front of a metal door with a NO ENTRY sign. I stare at the butterfly, once again trapped in my fear, and my chest tightens with disbelief. The butterfly shines so brightly it becomes a blurred silver dot, and I have to squint to make out its shape.

It can't be real. It can't be real. Silver butterflies aren't real. It's impossible; the silver butterfly is a figment of my twisted imagination. A beautiful symbol of the ugly thoughts in my head.

But here it is right in front of me, more majestic and terrible than in my dreams.

It hovers in the air and moves in small circles, like it's trying to get me to follow. "This can't be happening, this can't be happening," I whisper, and back away from the butterfly.

All this time I wanted to confront my monster, but now that part of my nightmare is right in front of me, there's no way I'm going to follow that butterfly.

I move away from the butterfly, and it flies through the air with astonishing speed. But when I turn to continue toward the twisted trees, it's right in front of me! And it darts at my eyes.

I yelp and race away from the area, half screaming, half

gasping, and you can guess what happens next . . . I trip over a vine and land hard on my chest, but manage to protect my face with my hands. I cower on the ground, waiting for another attack from—

From a butterfly? The realization hits me in the face with a slap. I'm running from something I could crush with a sneeze. I'm not trapped in a dream right now; this is reality and I'm in control.

With renewed confidence, and a little embarrassment, I get to my feet, dust off my jeans, and check on the camera equipment in my bag. I'm sure there's a reasonable explanation for that butterfly; maybe I saw a picture of it in one of Dad's books when I was younger, and it just happened to manifest in my nightmare?

I've fallen into a circle of coconut trees that shoot into the air among small shrubs, so tall I can't see the top. But these trees were planted by humans; no trees grow in a perfect circle with the exact same distance between them.

After taking one last check around for the butterfly, I follow a row coconut trees, pushing through several plants and bushes. The forest is getting drier and drier, with brown taking over the green, though the soil gets muddier by the second.

Then, after pushing away a cluster of leaves, I spy a small path through some dead bushes, big enough for a young child to crawl through. I squeeze through the bush, spitting leaves from my mouth, and then I see a glorious sight in the distance.

A towering gray fence.

With a strangled sob, I race toward it. I'm finally here! I did it! My parents are going to be furious, but it's all going to be worth it when I see the excitement on Peace's face and get more footage for my film.

I rush toward the fence, thinking about his small smile, a warm bath, and a hot meal.

Then all the music in the air disappears.

TAKE 9—DON'T SCREAM

I forgot how lifeless the world is without sound.

It's like there's water trapped in my ears. The white noise of the trees, the chattering of dry leaves—it's all gone. I rub my ears, hoping to pop the stillness, but the atmosphere remains dead.

I halt in my tracks, afraid to go closer. I can't make out much beyond the fence, but no decent hotel would let the bush grow wild and untamed around the property like this.

But what's the alternative? Go back through the forest to find a place with music?

I check my phone again, but there's still no signal. I don't have a choice; maybe someone inside can give me directions. I pry the iPod out of my jeans and breathe a sigh of relief when the spouge blasts in my ears. The music gives me the courage to move closer.

The back of a tall gray building comes into view, with two giant satellite dishes on top of a shiny glass roof.

I've never seen a building that spoke to me before, much less with threatening words. It has reflective glass doors, but there are no windows, except at the very top. It clashes with the inviting white picnic tables and bright-green fake grass surrounding it.

The tall fence seems to be pushing the forest away. The barbed wire at the top of the fence has a row of strange black boxes with metal rods that protrude from the middle and narrow to a sharp point, with small gray globes near the top. They look like military Q-tips.

I remember the Captain's warning: *This place doesn't like uninvited guests.*

"Hello?" I call. A light on one of the black devices comes on and starts to flicker. I wave in case it's a camera, but nothing happens.

I remove the headphones and the silence slams into my ears so hard I get an instant headache. I wince but manage to let out a timid, "Hello, is anyone there?"

I push my headphones back in my ears and walk along the fence, humming lyrics and searching for a sign or a gate. Then I come to an abrupt stop. There's someone by the picnic table inside the facility.

A boy.

He looks about my age, though slightly taller. His brown skin is in desperate need of cocoa butter, and dark circles swallow his eyes. But his face is as gray as his long tunic and slacks, and his mouth hangs open as he stares at me. I pull the headphones from my ears.

"Elijah?" he whispers. With a trembling hand, he brings an inhaler from his pocket, takes a puff, and gets ready to run.

"Wait!" I cry. A few more lights flicker along the fence.

"You speak!" he exclaims. The sound of the boy's voice startles me . . . because it has an actual sound, not the just-above-whisper tone.

The boy cowers and looks around apologetically to no one. I know that feeling. In fact, I am best friends and worst enemies with that feeling.

"Who are you?" he asks, glancing at the top of the fence. "Don't come any closer," he warns when I step nearer to it.

"Okay, I swear I'm not a murderer or anything. Though if I *were* a murderer, I wouldn't admit it," I say with a small laugh.

This isn't going very well. The boy gets ready to bolt again.

"Wait! I just need some directions to the silent retreat. Is it close by?"

"Retreat?" The boy cocks his head. "As far as I know, there's nothing on this island but the clinic." He unclips a radio from his belt.

"Clinic?" That can't be right.

A horrible thought dawns on me. Suppose the retreat got canceled at the last minute and my parents didn't come to Duppy Island after all?

I groan. "Omigod, I'm in so much trouble; my parents are going to kill me. No, Peace is going to kill me."

"Peace? You're Peace's sister? Serenity?" The boy lowers the radio and examines my face.

"Yeah, that's me," I say in surprise. "Do I know you?"

"No. Peace mentioned you earlier, when I asked about his paints." He pauses and lowers his voice. "You have to leave. It's not safe."

My chest tightens at his eerie warning. "What do you mean? Is my brother okay?"

Without thinking, I walk right up to the fence and press my face against it but then realize it could be electric. I brace myself for a shock, but thankfully nothing happens.

"It's not safe for *you*," the boy replies. "You're not allowed—wait, how did you get here anyway?"

"I hiked through the forest." I pluck a branch from my hair. "And where is *here*? What kind of place is this?" *And why is there no sound?*

"Through the forest?" He glances at the area behind me with fearful eyes. "You're not supposed to go into the bushes. It's against the rules."

"Well, it's too late for that now," I reply, gesturing at the bits of forest all over my body.

"Did you see anything out there? Or anyone?"

"I'm not answering any more of your questions until you answer mine."

He blows out air. "I told you: This is a medical facility. Peace is with Dr. Whisper now." The boy nervously taps the radio with a fingernail—it sounds like someone rattling a jammed doorknob. "He's going to be so mad."

"Who is this Dr. Whisper everyone keeps talking about?" I demand, remembering Eloise's mother mentioned him at the dock. "And why is he with my brother?"

Jacob shrugs. "Maybe for medical reasons? He *is* a doctor, you know."

I have too many questions racing through my head to be bothered by his sarcasm. Why would Peace need medical treatment? He's never been ill a day in his life. My parents have never once hinted Peace had a medical condition, and he's never shown any signs of . . . my heart stops when I remember his silent music. Does it disappear because he's sick?

"Why would they not tell me?" I ask, more to myself than the boy. "Exactly what kind of doctor is this Dr. Whisper?"

The radio crackles and we both jump at the sound of the Captain's gruff voice.

"Come in, Dr. Whisper, this is the Captain speaking. Over."

His eyes widen and he grips the radio. "He's going to contact the clinic next if I don't answer."

"Please, don't let anyone else know I'm here," I beg. "I want to find out what's going on with Peace first."

"I'm sorry, there's nowhere to hide."

"Pleeeeease."

The boy sighs and looks up to the sky. Then he presses a button on the radio. "This is Jacob. Dr. Whisper's busy with a client. Over."

"A young girl was headed to your location. Did she arrive? Over."

I continue to plead to Jacob with my eyes. He's silent for a few seconds but then presses the button again.

"She's here safe and sound. You can continue on as scheduled. Over and out." He turns off the radio.

A swirl of emotions erupts inside me. I'm not accustomed to anyone besides Peace having my back, especially strangers. I reach through the fence and squeeze his hand in appreciation. He seems startled by my touch, and then his whole face brightens so much he looks like a different person. I wish I could hear his music.

"Thank you! Thank you so—"

"Shhhhhhh."

I'm a little disappointed; I don't need another shusher in my life.

Jacob points to the black devices on the fence. "Sound meters. The alarm goes off for anything more than fifty decibels."

I want to laugh, but that would set off the alarm. "What happens if it goes off?"

"I don't want to know," Jacob says with a shiver. He

beckons for me to follow and we walk along the fence, toward the creepy building.

"I still don't understand," I say, trying to imagine what might be wrong with Peace. "Is Dr. Whisper a surgeon? A psychiatrist—what?"

"Um, I dunno," he replies, sticking his palms in the air. "A pediatrician, I guess? I've only ever seen kids go in the clinic."

"Isn't he your doctor too?"

"Nah, my dad just got the caretaker job, so Mum sent me and my brothers here for the summer. I was excited till I found out there's no TV or Wi-Fi. Some vacation," he grumbles.

I was expecting a gate, but we reach the very end of the fence near the awful cement building and there's nothing but white, jagged rocks.

"This is your best way in," the boy says, pointing up at the fence against the rock. It's much lower and there are no sound meters at the top.

I take my time scaling the fence, but on my way down one of my feet slips in my awkward attempt to avoid the pointy, sharp bits at the top, and I land on my backside. I open my mouth to cry out but Jacob presses his hand against my lips.

"Don't. Scream," he warns, his eyes on the closest sound meter.

I nod, and water builds up in my eyes from biting my tongue. Jacob removes his hand and helps me to my feet.

"I doubt my parents will let me stick around, so I need to stay hidden for as long as possible. Is that the clinic?" I point to the gray building.

Jacob nods.

My stomach turns at the thought of Peace inside that creepy place. If there's something seriously wrong with my brother, then I should be in there with him.

"Can you sneak me in and—"

"Are you insane? Absolutely not," Jacob hisses. "Look, when your brother comes out, I'll bring him to you. This way."

I pause for a second but then reluctantly follow him across the lawn. We hurry past the picnic table and squeeze through a small space between the gray building and another wooden structure on short stilts that smells of stale roasted corn.

Jacob checks to make sure no one is around, and we slip out of the space and into the main facility.

It's definitely not the luxury resort I expected. First off, it's completely deserted. It reminds me of an empty street in Gran's village, with small wooden chattel houses in a semicircle. Normally chattel houses would be popping with oranges, purples, and greens, but these houses are all gray, as if the fog has eaten the color too. The only brightness comes from the startling fluorescent-green patches of fake grass between a gray tiled path snaking around the facility.

Jacob leads me to a galvanized hangar and inside the space

blimp from the beach. I'm disappointed that the interior looks like a regular commercial flight with overhead bins, but with crates in the seats instead of passengers.

"My father is coming to unload the airship soon."

"Is that what you call this? Is it a plane or a blimp?"

"A bit of both—a prototype. Dr. Whisper is well-connected." He pulls a gray tunic from an overhead bin. "You can change into this and hide under there." He points to a space under the back seat, where you'd put extra carry-on luggage.

"Don't worry, it's just until we finish unloading and do a spot check. Then you can stay here till I see Peace."

"Thank you, thank you, thank you." I grab the stiff cloth from his hands.

Jacob shuffles out of the airship, but then he stops in the doorway. "By the way, were you humming Draytons Two earlier?"

"You know spouge?" I've never met anyone my age who knew the musical group.

"Fun fact," Jacob says, tilting his chin. "Did you know Jackie Opel's voice was so loud, he could turn his back to the mic and perform a song?"

"Yup. Fun fact. Did you know his voice was so loud, he would sing to people on the top deck of a cruise ship from the ocean?"

"Yup."

Jacob and I grin at each other, and suddenly it's like I've reconnected with an old friend.

"Man, I'm sorry you have to leave," he says, and then after a pause, he looks me dead in the eye. "You sure you didn't see anything in the forest? Nothing strange happened?"

I think about the weird musical bush and the silver butterfly and feel the urge to tell him about them. But then I would have to explain my ability to hear people's music, and I'm not about to share something so personal with a stranger.

"No, nothing at all," I reply, shrugging.

Jacob seems unconvinced, but he nods and shuts the door, leaving my lie lingering in the air.

TAKE 10—MEET THE PERFECT CHILDREN

I am a human pretzel.

From under the seat, with my cheek smashed against the floor, I watch gray Crocs and sneakers walk up and down the aisle. Jacob's father's heels remind me of the Captain's. Hard and crusty.

To distract myself from the pain, I pretend to be a contestant on one of those survival game shows, performing a stunt where I'm suspended in midair and have to stay in position until the timer goes off.

I close my eyes and imagine the score for the scene. Definitely a rock beat, maybe with angsty electric guitar riffs.

I'm so caught up in my daydream I don't realize I'm mimicking the rolling noise of bass drums at the back of my throat, making me the loudest stowaway on the planet.

"Why, hello there!"

I open my eyes to see a wide jovial face in front of mine. He has the expression of someone about to deliver the punch line to a joke.

I crawl out from under the seat, hot with shame. Jacob raises his palms in the air and mouths, *Seriously?* But he recovers quickly.

"Did you find your earring?" Jacob asks, his eyes urging me to follow his lead. "She was just checking under the seats," he explains to his father.

Jacob's dad cocks his head. "You look familiar."

I cast a frantic glance at Jacob, afraid to say the wrong thing.

Jacob jumps in. "Dad, this is Serenity. You met her earlier, remember? She said 'Cry Me a River' was her favorite record, and you told her to call you Uncle Newton."

I nod, mouth too dry to respond.

Uncle Newton gives me a smile so bright it almost makes up for not hearing his music. "Ah yes, I remember! Good taste, good taste."

Both Jacob and I exhale, and he glares at me after Uncle Newton leaves with a crate.

"You're lucky he has a terrible memory," he snaps.

"What now?" I whisper.

"Just grab a crate and play along," he replies. "Not that one, that's mine," he says when I reach for a covered plastic crate with a FRAGILE sticker.

When I get outside, I peep at the gray building, hoping to see Peace coming through the door with his half smile, safe and sound. The front of the building is a mirror of the back, with the same reflective doors and windowless walls.

"These are the last ones," Jacob says, taking the crate from my hands and carefully resting it on the ground.

"Good, good, let's go. We don't want to miss the opening." Uncle Newton guides us out of the hangar.

"Wait, Dad, Serenity is starving. I promised her something to eat first," Jacob says, trying to pull away. He gestures his head toward the clinic and we exchange panicked looks.

"No time, no time. And I told you to call me Newton. 'Dad' is so old-fashioned."

"You *are* old-fashioned," Jacob replies in an exasperated manner. Any other day I would have laughed.

Thankfully the courtyard is still empty. I turn my face away and keep my head down as we pass the mirrored doors. If my parents catch me at the facility now, I'll be back on a boat before I figure out what's going on.

"The rest of the gang was in the common room practicing some psychedelic moves before I left." Uncle Newton taps his fingers together with glee.

Psychedelic? Someone is stuck in the seventies. Next to me, Jacob rolls his eyes and shakes his head, and I stifle a laugh.

Uncle Newton leads us toward a large building in the

center of the chattel houses, with a thatched roof made of coconut fronds so aged the leaves are almost white instead of green.

"A nice girl like you will fit right in. How old are you?" Uncle Newton asks, cutting across a grassy area with an identical white picnic table.

"I just turned twelve."

"Ah! Twelve is a special age. Not many children reach it." I glance up at him, but his face is so cheerful I must have misheard.

I survey the space. "This place is a ghost town," I whisper to Jacob.

"Most children are gone now; it's only me, my brothers, and the Glitches left."

"The Glitches?"

He gives me a knowing look. "You'll see."

The building looks like it's about to collapse. Uncle Newton hops up the rotting wooden steps, and I pause, expecting them to give way beneath him, but nothing happens. Nothing. Not even a creak.

I tentatively place a foot on the step, and to my surprise, it is cement. Sculpted and painted to resemble insect-ridden wood.

"Let's just get this over with." Jacob waits at the top for me. "They get upset if you're late."

The inside of the thatched house is deceiving as well. Polished cement walls, all sculpted to look like aged wood, and tiled floors. It resembles a large studio with dance wall-paper and chairs precisely laid out around the perimeter, already prepped for an audience.

But there's no one here except Uncle Newton and two brown-skinned, cheeky-looking twin boys, who also look about the same age as Peace. Jacob sits next to the twins, close to the entrance, but he stops me when I try to sit in the chair beside him. He removes a white tack that is almost invisible on the plastic chair and glares at the two boys, who cover their mouths and giggle.

"My brothers, John and James—don't bother, I can hardly tell the difference between them. Actually I doubt they even know who is who," Jacob whispers. "They're always trying to make you set off the sound alarm."

A loud shush comes from Uncle Newton, and seconds after, Jacob's brothers imitate him. What's the big deal? The show hasn't even started.

But then the gray wallpaper begins to twitch at the back of the room. That's when I realize the five figures are real humans in gray leotards and leggings, and not part of the decor. They are all the same height and size, just a little taller than Peace: same thin lips, button noses, and dark brown eyes, with their black hair up in tight buns. They would be copy-and-paste identical, except their skin tones are various shades of brown, from light to dark.

Then they seem to pop out of the wall, scurrying to the

middle of the room and striking different poses that appear to defy gravity.

The quintuplets start to dance, leaping all over the room in movements somewhere between ballet and being burned alive. And there's no music, though that doesn't stop Uncle Newton from conducting with an invisible baton and Jacob's brothers from bobbing their heads.

"Is the Glitches their stage name?" I ask Jacob.

"No, but don't they look like a malfunction?" Jacob murmurs with feigned interest on his face. "I'm still trying to figure out who is the original copy."

I try not to laugh, but it makes sense. If it wasn't for the different skin tones, I would have been convinced they were all one person. Even their facial expressions are identical. I wonder what their music would be like. Maybe the swoosh of paper shuffling out of a printer.

The Glitches bow, and everyone taps their index fingers together in "applause." Together, the Glitches pit-a-pat up to us.

"Will you dance with me?" they whisper at the same time.

Uncle Newton and the boys leap from their seats and start to do a two-step around the room. Jacob sighs and pulls out his inhaler. He takes a quick puff, then gets to his feet and does a reluctant bounce on the spot. Uncle Newton beckons for me to join them on the dance floor and does an exaggerated shoulder roll.

As I gape at them dancing in silence, I can't help but

notice how the Glitches and both of Jacob's brothers remind me of Peace.

Something's not right. First no one in the facility has music; there's just never-ending silence in the air. There aren't many people around, except these strange kids in a fake-rotting building. No sign of my brother or my parents yet. It's like I'm trapped in the beginning of a low-budget horror movie.

Suddenly I get a desperate urge to hear Mum's soft clucking noises and for Dad to hold me against his white dashiki shirt and ruffle my hair. I need to confront them and find out what's going on. Give them a chance to explain why they lied. For the first time, I want to see them shake their heads at my growing concerns and give me a rational explanation for this creepy place.

I get to my feet and do an awkward jig over to Jacob.

"I changed my mind," I whisper to him. "I want to talk to my mum and dad. They're in the clinic with Peace, right?"

He turns to me with confusion. "What are you talking about? Parents aren't allowed on Duppy Island."

TAKE 11—DON'T TELL

"You're lying!"

I can't hide the panic in my voice. Everyone except Jacob shushes me, but I don't care.

My parents would not leave Peace by himself on a strange, secluded island, especially if he's sick. But then again, I never thought they would abandon me and pretend to go on a family vacation either.

Something outside catches Uncle Newton's attention. "Ah, here comes Dr. Whisper now."

Jacob's alarmed eyes meet mine. "If the doctor sees you, you're gone."

There's no way I will leave Peace alone on this strange island with these bizarro kids. Jacob shifts his gaze to the exit and both of us inch toward the door. Luckily, Uncle Newton and the others are so engrossed in the "dance party," we're able to slip away.

My heart pounds while we rush down the hallway. We hop through a window at the end of the corridor and dart around the back of the building. We use the chattel houses for cover until we duck underneath the house that reeks of stale corn.

Jacob exhales and slumps against the L-shaped bricks. "I'm sorry, but—"

I brace myself for the scolding. If I could have kept quiet for five minutes in the blimp, we wouldn't be in this mess.

"This is the most fun I've had in a while." He takes another quick puff of his inhaler but then loses his smile when he sees my face. "What?"

"What do you mean no parents are allowed? Your father is here."

"He's staff; he doesn't count. But I've been here a month, and parents normally drop off children from the beach and then pick them up a few days later."

I sit up. "Lemme get this straight. You've been here for almost a month, and you've never been inside the clinic?"

He shrugs. "If I needed an appointment, Dad would have made one, like he did for my brothers."

"Why would your brothers need treatment from Dr. Whisper?"

He hesitates, but then words come tumbling out, as if he's been holding them in for a long time.

"They're awful! They've always been practical jokers, but now . . ." He shudders. "They started seeing Dr. Whisper around their birthday last month, when they turned six years

old, and their jokes got more and more cruel . . . and dangerous. Now Dad can't stop talking about how better-behaved
my brothers are." He pauses. "I'm still removing tacks from my
bed every day."

"So, you don't think Dr. Whisper's treatment is helping
your brothers?" I ask.

Jacob stiffens and he avoids my eyes. "I never said that."

"You implied it."

"I did not. Stop putting words in my mouth."

I lean closer. "You're afraid of Dr. Whisper, aren't you? Is
my brother safe here?"

Jacob takes a deep breath. "Listen, let's focus on the original plan. Wait here, and as soon as the coast is clear, I'll
bring Peace to you. Trust me, this place isn't so bad. Today's
show was a little weird, but we have movie nights, sports,
games—we can't breach the sound limit, of course, or leave
the compound."

I admit it seems like the best plan . . . for now. Jacob
exhales as I lean back against the bricks and bring my knees
to my chest. I glance over at the surrounding trees and
remember the musical bush.

"Are there a lot of silver butterflies on the island?"

"I haven't even seen a mosquito, much less a butterfly."

"No mosquitoes?" That doesn't make any sense, not while
we're surrounded by foliage. "Not even in the forest?"

Jacob's eyes widen. "No one's allowed—"

"I know, I know." I cut him off. "It's against the rules."

"Seriously, it's dangerous out there." He looks out at the forest and shudders. "Things live in the bushes."

"Douens?"

Jacob stares at me in horror.

"What do you know about them?" I press. "Besides the fact that they have no faces and backward feet."

"I don't want to talk about them."

"Pleeeease," I beg again, leaning forward.

Jacob folds his arms, but I can tell he wants to say more, despite his reluctance. "I heard they're really intelligent, especially knowledgeable in medicine. And sometimes they have different tribes. The brown ones are harmless, but the red douens are tricksters and could be trouble."

I tilt my head. "You seem to know a lot about douens."

"Read about them in a book called *The Treasure Chest of African and Caribbean Folklore*. There're creatures similar to douens in Ghana called mmoatia."

I take note of it for my movie—could be a good twist. "Have you ever seen these faceless children?"

"I'm not talking about it."

There's silence, and I arch my eyebrows.

Jacob soon gives in again. "I've never seen them in the flesh, but there was a boy. Elijah." He lowers his voice. "I think he went into the forest and never came back."

My stomach churns at the idea of someone's little brother

lost in the forest. "That's horrible! What did the police say?"

"I dunno." Jacob gives a solemn look. "No one went looking for him."

"What? Isn't that illegal?" I ask, getting frustrated. "So you don't know about mysterious sound alarms or the lack of insects or the treatments. Do you know anything at all?"

He stares at me until I start to fidget under the scrutiny. "Do you know what those lyrics mean? The ones you were humming earlier."

"You mean, 'yuh come here fuh drink milk, or yuh come here fuh count cow'?"

"Fun fact. It means, don't worry about things that don't concern you." This time there's no humor in his voice. "I keep my head down and mind my own business."

Suddenly there's movement ahead. From this angle, I can see the lower halves of people gathering in the courtyard. Multiple pairs of feet in gray ballet shoes and gray Crocs.

Jacob gasps and starts to crawl out from under the cellar. "I forgot about evening meditation! They'll come looking for me."

"Please don't take long," I beg. "I don't wanna be here by myself when it gets dark."

Jacob looks at me the same way my dad did when he caught me making fake blood in the kitchen. "You *really* don't know anything about this place. Serenity, it doesn't get dark here."

He scrambles away before I can get clarification.

Everyone lines up in a circle along the tiles and starts to walk very, very slowly around the compound. After a few steps, all the feet pause at the same time. I catch my breath, wondering if I accidentally made a noise. But then everyone continues around the courtyard again. They repeat the same walk-stop routine, like the world's laziest army.

And without a sound.

There's definitely something wrong with this island . . . this place. People don't just lose their music. It's not a pencil in a pocket or an umbrella on a bus. It would be like walking into a building and coming out without an arm. And the horrible thing is, no one but me would notice the limb was missing.

I put in my headphones, grateful that I didn't leave them on the airship with my backpack.

After about ten minutes, I notice a familiar set of feet and relief floods my chest. I'm sure I know those feet. I shove my headphones back into my pocket, get on all fours, and scurry over to the other end of the structure.

More of his body comes into my view. Black slacks, slim hands, gray tunic, and finally, a small head. It takes all my self-control not to call out.

It *is* Peace!

I can't stop myself from crawling out from under the house, despite Jacob's warning.

I almost bowl Peace over in front of a bathroom stall.

"Oh, thank God, I was so worried!" I whisper in his ear. But he doesn't return my hug. He's as stiff as a board and his arms remain limp at his sides.

I pull away and gaze into his face, desperate to see his rare full smile and excited eyes, but instead, his expression is as blank as an empty canvas.

I grab his shoulders and bring my face closer to his. "Ace, what's wrong?" I watch as a tiny light of recognition comes into his eyes.

"Ren?" he whispers, and touches my cheek, as if to make sure I'm not a hallucination. "What are you doing here?"

"Don't worry about me." I tilt Peace's face upward, pressing my palm against his forehead. "Are you sick?"

Peace shakes his head, and I release a huge breath. Then I take both his hands in mine. They're warm, though it's chilly outside. "Then why did Mum and Dad bring you here?"

My heart drops when he says with a small voice, "I haven't seen my parents in a long time."

I pull him into another hug, and tears flow down my cheeks. This time he makes a weak attempt to return it. "Don't worry, I'm going to find them." Maybe I can persuade Jacob to contact them or the coast guard or even the Captain. I need to stay hidden a bit longer so I can radio for help.

I wipe my eyes with the backs of my hands. "Don't tell

anyone you saw me. Okay? Stay close to Jacob and he'll bring you to me later."

Peace bites his lip and nods, then looks past my shoulder. I check behind me, but no one's there. Still, it's time to get back into hiding.

"Don't tell anyone," I whisper, and then give him a gentle nudge toward the courtyard. He hurries away, and I wait for him to look back for one last glance, but he doesn't turn around.

Before returning to the cellar, I realize I need to go.

I push open the cracked bathroom door with my pinkie, but thankfully, inside is neat and clean. A minute later, the flush sounds like a river flowing across polished rocks. Not even the toilet is allowed to be loud.

I scoff in disgust, and when I open the door I collide into a tall, muscled figure.

Dr. Whisper.

Peace steps out from behind him and points a finger right at me.

TAKE 12—DR. WHISPER

Have you ever wished life was a movie set and you could yell "Cut!" and have a chance to do it all over again?

Yeah, me too.

It feels like my soul tore itself from my body to observe the scene. Some other Serenity has a brother who betrayed her. That Serenity is in big trouble.

Dr. Whisper is surprisingly beautiful. No, beautiful isn't the right word—maybe robotic or synthetic? His face is so angular it could be built with Legos. As I take in his shiny bald head and white jacket, a shock of recognition goes through me.

Dr. Whisper is the man on the dock with the awful music! I glance at Peace and then back to the doctor in horror. Someone with such a menacing sound shouldn't be trusted with vulnerable people, especially my brother.

"Good day, how can I help you?"

His voice seems polite, but I know better. I've heard his music. I swallow the giant ball of fear in my throat and attempt to peer around Dr. Whisper's towering form for Jacob.

Dr. Whisper shifts his body, forcing me to meet his gaze. "May I ask how you got into this facility?"

I'm not sure how to answer without implicating Jacob. I glance at Peace for help, and his look of shame sends a pang through my heart. Dr. Whisper probably saw us by the bathroom and forced him to confess.

"It's impolite to ignore a direct question." This time, Dr. Whisper's eyes betray him, flashing with anger for a fleeting second. He takes a step toward me, and I get ready to grab Peace and run.

"It's time to boogie!" a voice sings.

Everyone turns to see Uncle Newton trying to bump hips with an annoyed Jacob. When he spots me by the stall with Dr. Whisper, Jacob leaps so high into the air he seems to levitate for a few seconds.

"Stephanie! You missed the end of the show." Uncle Newton's voice trails away and his smile drops when he senses the tension.

Dr. Whisper presses his lips together in a thin line and his eye twitches. "You brought this girl here, Mr. Newton?"

"No, well, I don't know," Uncle Newton responds, uncertain. "She was on the flight, right, son?"

He glances at Jacob for confirmation, who starts to wither under the pressure. Dr. Whisper flares his perfect nostrils and switches his gaze between me and Jacob. He's about to confess; I can't let him get into trouble because of me.

"I hid on the ferry, then snuck onto the blimp when everyone was distracted," I blurt.

There's silence. I flick my eyes to the ground so he can't see the truth inside them.

"Mr. Newton, contact the Captain," Dr. Whisper commands. Uncle Newton flinches as if he's being disciplined as well. "I want her gone."

Uncle Newton looks at me with pity and then heads toward the blimp. Jacob seems torn between chasing after him to cover up his lie and staying to make sure I don't rat him out.

I muster up some courage and grab Peace's hand. "I'm not leaving without my brother, and not until I speak to my parents. Where are they?"

Dr. Whisper stares at me until I feel myself shrinking inside, getting smaller and smaller until I'm no bigger than a speck of dirt under his shoes.

"Your parents are getting some much-needed rest, and your brother needs special counseling. I cannot have you interfering with my treatment, especially at such a sensitive time for Peace."

Much-needed rest? Did my parents travel to a silent retreat on another island? I know they've been exhausted, but I just can't swallow that they'd leave Peace alone here, especially if he's unwell. My alarm bells go off again.

"But what special counseling? There's nothing wrong with my brother."

Dr. Whisper raises a sculpted eyebrow. "So you think it's completely normal to be paralyzed with fear at night?"

I am speechless. Surely my parents didn't go through all this trouble because of Peace's new fear of the dark? There are dozens of counselors he could have visited at home.

"Take her to the common room until we sort out transportation off the island," Dr. Whisper says to Jacob.

I draw the reluctant Peace closer and stand my ground. "If you make me leave, I'll tell the police you kidnapped my brother." I pull my phone from my pocket, even though there's still no signal.

Dr. Whisper narrows his eyes and I try to maintain my defiant gaze.

Uncle Newton appears with my backpack and breaks the standoff.

"Captain said he just docked in Saint Lucia and isn't coming back till Friday." That's three days away.

Peace's birthday.

If my parents *did* arrange for Peace to stay at the facility, then surely they'd return by then. They would not let him spend his birthday here alone.

Dr. Whisper scowls. "Then charter a private plane. We can charge it to her parents' account."

I step forward. "Wait, please." My parents could barely

81

afford the ferry. I would never forgive myself if they have to sell the house to pay off this debt. Worse, I don't know if they would ever forgive me. "I promise I'll be quiet. You won't even know I'm here."

Dr. Whisper surveys me, and then some kind of lightbulb goes off in his head.

"Miss Noah," he finally says, tapping his chin. "If you're going to stay with us, you need to make yourself useful. You can assist with the laundry, tend to the grass, and clean all the rooms."

I open my mouth to protest, but Jacob gives me a warning look.

"And you need to be acquainted with the rules. First, no loud noises. Anything over fifty decibels is unacceptable."

I nod and pretend I'm hearing it for the first time.

"You are not allowed in the clinic, and anywhere outside the fence is out-of-bounds. Going into the forest is strictly forbidden."

Dr. Whisper snatches my phone from my hands so suddenly I don't have time to react. His fingertips are ice-cold and unexpectedly rough, like sandpaper.

He continues, "The third rule. No recording equipment of any kind."

He rips open my bag and starts rifling through my things. Dr. Whisper finds my camera and dangles it on his glacier finger by the string, as if it is something dirty.

"Wait, I wanted, I wanted—" I pause, fighting back panic. I doubt he would care about my horror film, but I can't give up my camera. "I wanted to shoot a nature documentary. About the silver butterflies."

There is a flash of emotion on Dr. Whisper's plastic face. Surprise? And then curiosity? It's so hard to read his features.

"The *Anima montium*," Dr. Whisper says, now looking at me with interest, "is extinct."

"It can't be. I—" I stop talking mid-sentence. I can't admit that I already broke the rule about going into the forest.

After he's satisfied there's no more contraband, Dr. Whisper throws my backpack at me.

"What happens if you break a rule?" I ask. Jacob and Uncle Newton exchange a worried look.

A small smirk appears on Dr. Whisper's face. He's looking forward to whatever punishment it would entail.

Dr. Whisper doesn't answer. "It is time to finish our session," he says, offering a hand to Peace.

I grab at him, but Peace slips away and accepts Dr. Whisper's outstretched hand.

"I'll be here when you're done," I promise him, but Peace doesn't acknowledge me, not even with his half smile.

Instead he turns away and leads Dr. Whisper toward the eerie clinic.

TAKE 13—PEACE'S STORY

I don't trust this Dr. Whisper person at all. It's still hard to believe my parents left Peace alone for some vague treatment at a facility on a deserted island. I need to find a way to contact Mum and Dad so they can confirm the story themselves.

After waiting in the common room for hours, I beg Uncle Newton to check on Peace and ask if I can send a message to my gran.

"She's probably worried about me," I say, pretending to be a responsible kid. I plan to call my parents instead to confirm Dr. Whisper's story.

"That shouldn't be a problem," Uncle Newton replies, stacking up the chairs. "I think you get one phone call."

I raise an eyebrow. "One phone call? Is this a prison?"

Uncle Newton beams at me and doesn't reply. "Time to peace out," he says, and shuffles everyone out the door.

Jacob gets a food crate from the airship and offers to help me settle in.

We walk past a house with blacked-out windows and turn at the chattel house next door with a patchy lattice border and stairs that seem to be infested with wood ants. I step onto the stairs and find that everything is made of cement.

Nothing on this island is as it seems. Maybe this is one of those slum-tourism experiences, where people pay a ton of money to pretend they're living on some poverty-stricken island.

The inside is much more luxurious than its downtrodden exterior would suggest. Unlike a regular chattel house, which has a separate living room, dining room, and kitchen, there's an open plan with a matching wrought iron living room and dining room set.

"Home sweet home." Jacob rests the crate gently on the kitchen counter.

I bounce on the spot. "Which one's the bathroom?" I ask, scanning the two doors in the short hallway.

"You know where they are," Jacob says, pointing at the stalls through the window. Then he gets a metal potty from under the sink. "For late-night emergencies."

He has *got* to be joking. The urge to pee leaves me immediately.

"And this is to collect water from the standpipe." He pulls a bucket from under the kitchen sink.

My mouth falls open in shock. "There's no running water

in the house?" That's when I realize why the space seemed so empty. There are no large appliances; no fridge or freezer, no TV—just a tiny gas stove in the corner.

"And no electricity either," Jacob says sadly.

"No power anywhere?" I scan the room and don't see any electrical outlets, not even light switches. They're carrying this tourist experience way too far.

"Dad says there's electricity in the clinic; it's solar-operated."

I check my iPod. Fifteen percent. Like all good film-makers, I had packed an external battery charger, but I only have enough charge to last a day if I use it sparingly.

"What's the matter?" Jacob asks, noticing my shaking hands.

"I . . . I can't survive here without my music."

Jacob's face softens. "Would singing help? The bedrooms are soundproof."

I go to check them out, mainly because I don't want him to see me cry.

The first room is sparse, with two single beds and a dresser. Peace's canvas and art supplies are scattered on the bed in the far-right corner. The room at the end of the hall has the same layout but with one double bed.

I'm about to step inside the larger bedroom when Uncle Newton enters the living room with Peace in his arms. Peace looks so small on his shoulder; his face is bent in vexation.

"What happened to my brother?" I demand.

Uncle Newton puts a finger to his lips, but I refuse to back down. I've never seen Peace look so weak. His hands flop around at his sides like they have no bones. I have to tell my parents about this.

"Uncle Newton, did you bring my phone? Can I contact my par— I mean, my gran?"

He shushes me again and places Peace on the bed. I exhale in frustration. It's clear I won't get any answers from him. I'll have to find another way to contact them myself.

Some of the knots in my stomach unravel when Peace sighs and snuggles into his pillow. Maybe he's just really tired.

I follow Uncle Newton into the kitchen, and my belly rumbles at the sight of canned food, bread, and a chunk of cheese.

"I have to go feed my brothers before they burn down the house," Jacob says.

"They're always trying new recipes," Uncle Newton adds, puffing out his chest with pride. "Such good boys." Jacob rolls his eyes.

I look at the cheese on the counter. "How can we survive without a fridge? What about leftovers?"

"Food doesn't spoil here. It's the fresh island air," Jacob says. It still doesn't make sense to me, but I'm too hungry and tired to argue, so I let them leave without questioning it.

"Oh, I almost forgot." Uncle Newton pops back inside and puts a small washcloth and a bottle of liquid soap on the table.

"It's okay," I say. "I brought my own."

"No, Dr. Whisper said you have to use these to mop and polish the grass tomorrow."

"Mop and *polish* the grass?" I repeat incredulously.

"Yup, every single blade. Should be a wicked workout," he says, and closes the door.

I sigh and start to make a sandwich, but then decide to collect drinking water and take a shower first. I tiptoe into the bedroom with the bucket, and I'm surprised to find Peace awake and playing with paper people on his bed. He looks up at me, his face expressionless, like he's dreaming with his eyes open.

I touch his forehead. "Ace, you're burning up!" What sort of counseling makes someone so tired? "Tell me what happened with Dr. Whisper."

"Serenity, why are you so loud?" Peace asks, without changing his expression.

I am taken aback. He never uses my full name, and his voice is filled with disgust.

"Sorry, I didn't . . . you're probably still tired?" I study his face, but there's no emotion. "Look, about earlier with Dr. Whisper. It's okay, I'm not upset. Everything worked out. Just talk to me."

"Okay. Here's the story." Peace dangles the paper girl in his fingers and then places her on his lap.

"Once upon a time, there was a girl who lived with her

family in a beautiful house, with flowers and birds and trees," he starts.

Peace lines up the rest of the paper family on the bed. "The mother, father, and brother were happy, but the daughter was miserable. She didn't appreciate what she had. The girl whined and sulked every day until her family couldn't take it anymore and told her to leave. Mum told her that she didn't belong in the family and Dad agreed."

A chill passes through me, but I say nothing.

Peace lifts the paper daughter in my face and slowly rips it in half. "The little girl left, and the family realized they were much better off without her. They realized they never loved her. They threw away all her clothes and turned her bedroom into a playroom for their perfect son."

A huge lump forms in my throat, and the bucket slips out of my fingers. No one except us hears when it hits the ground. Sixty decibels.

"Everyone was glad she was gone and prayed that she would never come back. And they lived happily ever after. The end."

He lets the pieces of the paper daughter fall to the ground. Stabbing me in the heart would be less painful.

Peace rests the paper mother, father, and son on his pillow. "You'll soon learn, Serenity, that the scariest stories are true."

My ragged sniffles fill the silence. Peace's blank expression never changes; he's shattered me and doesn't even care enough to sweep up the pieces.

I grab the bucket and race outside, leaning against the front door as I wipe away my tears. Whatever they are, Dr. Whisper's treatments are having a horrible effect on Peace. My brother has never been so mean, not to me or anyone. I need to talk to my parents and beg them to find another counselor.

It's almost six and the already gray sky turns a darker shade of gray, like it can sense my sour mood. There's no one else outside, not even crickets. I suddenly feel that strange urge again, a faint melody beckoning from the trees.

There is music out there, and it's getting stronger. The vines seem to curl around the fence like fingers, calling me to come closer.

I take a step toward it, and then there is a loud click. At least sixty decibels. Over the sound limit. The sound meters along the fence flash, and a blinding light floods the entire facility.

I shut my eyes and slam my hands over my ears. The light is so bright I can *hear* it in my head. Imagine being trapped in a screaming echo.

I dash back into the house, leaving the bucket behind.

TAKE 14—THE BLANK CANVAS

I sit up, drenched with sweat, the image of the silver butterfly still burned in my brain. I've never had my nightmare twice in one month.

I'm already reaching for the metal bowl under my bed when I realize two things: one, there's no nausea, and two, I'm not home.

I decided to sleep in the second bedroom after I bolted into the house last night. Apparently those awful lights come on automatically every day at six p.m. The linen curtains did nothing to block out the blinding-white glare last night. It was like putting a veil over the sun.

Those lights, along with the knife Peace shoved into my back, made it impossible to have a good night's rest.

I'm about to pull my hand from under the bed when it grazes against something cold and solid. I lift up the bed skirt and peer underneath.

Nothing but suitcases.

Green-and-brown suitcases.

I leap from the bed so fast, my foot becomes tangled in the sheets and I tumble onto the floor. I drag one of the suitcases from under the bed, and sure enough, I see Mum's stylish handwriting on the name tags.

My parents are here! They must've arrived while I was sleeping.

A huge weight lifts from my shoulders. I race out of the bedroom, ready to give them huge hugs, even though they'll most likely be mad I snuck onto the island. But I can deal with that later. All that matters now is convincing them to take us home. Once they see what Dr. Whisper's doing to Peace, they'll agree that something is seriously wrong here.

But there's no one in the house, not even Peace.

A thought dawns on me. My parents couldn't have arrived on the island in the middle of the night. They can't afford a private plane, and the next boat isn't coming until Friday. This means they've been somewhere at the facility all along. But where?!

Before I reach the front door, Dr. Whisper steps inside. He's changed from his long white coat into an identical gray one, and right now his gaze is almost as terrible as the music I heard on the beach. Suddenly the room seems as large as a shoebox.

"You missed meditation. It is from six to seven a.m."

More meditation? I wonder if this is part of his "special counseling."

"But I didn't know—"

"That's no excuse," Dr. Whisper replies, cutting me off, though his voice is half as loud as mine.

"As punishment, you can scrub the common room and the warren before you start on the grass . . . with this." He gives me an old toothbrush and leaves.

This man hates me and I don't understand why.

I dress quickly and try to check the time on my iPod. It's completely dead. I plug my iPod into the external charger for its last and only charge, then hurry to find my family.

My parents aren't in the courtyard or with the group of people by the standpipe.

Jacob scolds me when I join the line to collect water. "You have to follow the rules here. You can't just skip meditation because you don't like it."

"I was asleep!"

"Really?" He struggles to lift the heavy bucket. "Peace said you were awake but didn't feel like coming."

My mouth drops open, and I watch as my brother climbs the stairs to the common room carrying canvas and art supplies. No, Jacob must be mistaken; my brother doesn't lie.

"Have you seen my parents?" I ask.

"I told you, no parents are—"

I cut him off. "I saw their suitcases in the house. They're here."

Jacob gapes at me. "I—I guess I could have missed them?

I was busy when the airship landed yesterday. My brothers were mixing household cleaners to make a stink bomb," he replies. He's about to say something else when Dr. Whisper clears his throat behind us.

"I'll ask my dad," Jacob whispers, before scampering away.

Where could they be? The facility is way too small for our paths not to cross. Peace's awful story still haunts my thoughts. Is it possible my parents heard I snuck onto the island and are avoiding me? I hope Peace's tale about an unwanted daughter is fiction and not based on truth.

By the time I collect water, the courtyard is deserted. I'm about to join Peace when I notice a movement by the house with the blacked-out windows. It's Jacob. He checks to make sure no one is watching and then hops over the gate.

I wonder what that's about . . . but I don't have the time to speculate. I grab the "cleaning tools" and hurry to the common room.

Peace is working on a painting alone in a corner, the canvas blocking his face. The Glitches, in their gray tutus and tunics, lean over the counter at the back of the room, so close together that they look like linked paper people. One of them—the one with the shade closest to Dad's mahogany desk—notices me at the door, and though she doesn't make a sound, the rest of the Glitches all turn their heads toward me at the same time.

"Serenity." They say it like a statement, an instruction

you'd say to Siri. They move aside to reveal the bottom layer of a small vanilla cake with intricate pink-icing roses.

"Will you bake with me?" they sing.

That's when I notice instead of flour, eggs, sugar, and baking pans, on the table are several small buckets with gray sludge that smells like the lime chemical Dad sprinkles around the house to get rid of vermin. Two of the Glitches dip their hands in their bucket and bring out dripping gray gunk, slopping it onto paper plates.

"Oh, I was craving plaster of paris. It's so delicious," Jacob says, coming up behind me with a bowl full of paper and wire.

The Glitches giggle and huddle together, casting shy glances at Jacob. I guess he's the local stud here.

Jacob bends to my ear. "Newton said your parents are resting and need time to themselves. Maybe they're in the clinic?"

My stomach drops to my feet, and I blink away the sting of tears. My parents really are avoiding me. I knew they'd be upset I followed them, but ignoring my presence and leaving me at Dr. Whisper's mercy is just cruel.

Jacob points to his brothers, who are now at a table with balls of gray wool. "James and John claim they're making socks for my dad, so keep an eye out for needles." He sits at an empty table and starts to twist some wires together.

I glance at Peace, but he's still focused on his canvas. His eyes seem vacant, like he's painting in another world. Instead of engaging in a one-sided convo, I decide it's best to get started on cleaning before Dr. Whisper checks in.

"You can't be serious," Jacob says incredulously after I've been scrubbing the tiles for a few minutes.

"The doctor's orders." I dip the toothbrush into the water in the bucket.

"But that is a waste of time," Jacob replies.

"You're one to talk. What's *that* supposed to be? A scribble?" I ask, pointing at the twisted wire on the table.

He actually looks offended. "It's a papier-mâché man." He dunks a piece of paper into the white paste and wraps it around a hoop in the middle of the wire, forming a torso.

"Hmm, wire people would look interesting on film." I get a desperate longing for my camera. It's been a while since I've thought about horror movies, but I guess that happens when it feels like you're living in one.

To my surprise, Jacob perks up with interest. "I've always wanted to act in a movie! Wait—is it the, uh, mushy kind?" His face flushes with embarrassment.

I lift my chin up in the air. "Only if you think faceless children who steal faces are romantic. I do stop-motion horror."

"Ugh! Why are you so obsessed with douens?"

I prepare to defend my art, but then Jacob shoves a finger in the air. "I know, why not do a zombie movie, except they break-dance, like, with their limbs literally breaking off."

Jacob makes his papier-mâché man dance like a zombie and hums an upbeat spouge beat under his breath. I smile for the first time since I arrived on this wretched island. I bet his music would sound like mine—I wish I could hear it.

Then I think about papier-mâché zombies missing half their heads and body parts, and an angel's choir sings in my head. "Here's the story. We could call it *Fading Light of the Dead*, about zombies attracted to sunlight so people have to live their lives in the dark."

"Okay, I want to be part of this," he declares.

I sigh. "Too bad Dr. Whisper took my camera."

"Maybe Dad can persuade him to return it."

I raise the toothbrush and washcloth in the air. "By the time I finish these chores, the Captain will be back to take me home."

"So, how about I help you clean? Then we'll have more time to work on this movie."

I turn my head to the side, analyzing his hopeful face. I did travel here to make a film, until I got distracted by the whole missing parents/evil doctor saga.

I take another glance at Peace, still immersed in his painting, and also think about my parents relaxing in the clinic. Why should I be the only person suffering? I *could* brainstorm this new zombie movie with Jacob.

Jacob blurts, "Last week, I spent two hours with the Glitches staring at a crack in the tile. I need this."

I laugh. "Deal."

While Jacob goes off to get more cleaning supplies, I go to scrub the area near Peace and take a peek over his shoulder.

The canvas seems blank, but on second look, I notice globs of dried white paint on the canvas. Peace puts more white paint on the palette and moves the brush over the canvas in short, rough strokes.

"Oh, you could put a red flower in the middle," I suggest, taking the red tube from the box. "It would look so much bet—"

"Why don't you mind your own business," Peace snaps. "I wish you were dead!"

I drop the tube of paint in shock. He slaps the paintbrush against the canvas, then gathers up his art supplies and marches past Jacob out the door.

I watch him go with a mixture of hurt and confusion.

Peace and I have never fought before. Ever.

I gaze down at the white painting and then back up at Jacob. "There's something wrong with my brother."

TAKE 15—LITTLE BUNNY

There's no way Dr. Whisper is only doing normal counseling with Peace. He's doing something to change him—I know it.

I pace around the room while Jacob scrubs the floor. I'm too concerned about Peace to care about Dr. Whisper's pointless chores right now. The Glitches and Jacob's brothers decide to go swimming, so it's just me, Jacob, and my growing distress in the common room.

I stop pacing. "I want to check out the clinic."

Jacob gasps and then splutters. "Are you allergic to obeying rules?"

"Peace said really . . . hurtful things to me. This isn't like him. Be honest, Jacob. Did your brothers change after spending time with Dr. Whisper?"

Jacob blinks a couple of times and then slumps against the wall. "I found a needle in my cereal this morning."

"A what!"

"Shhhh!" Jacob eyeballs the sound meters through the window.

"Jacob." I lower my voice and move closer to him. "That. Is. Not. Normal."

"I was going to talk to Dad about it; they were never this bad," he admits, resigned. "But my brothers are so good at pretending to be angels when Newton is around." Then he shakes his head. "Maybe it's just . . . hypnosis gone wrong."

I roll my eyes. "Jacob, my parents' luggage is in their room, but no one has seen them—that's not normal either. I know you don't like to break rules, but there's something strange about that clinic. I'm taking a look inside, with or without you."

I start to gather up the toothbrush, washcloth, and bucket, hoping he doesn't call my bluff because I have no idea how to sneak in.

There's a long sigh behind me. "Newton always leaves his key card lying around in the warren. I doubt he'd notice if it was gone for a little while."

I whirl around. "I'm supposed to scrub the warren next! Um, what's a warren?"

"The bunny hut. That's Newton's domain," he says, emptying the bucket in the sink. "He doesn't care if it's dirty. We can pretend to clean and swipe the pass."

In his nervousness, Jacob finishes the rest of the room in record time. As we head outside, we pass another door and hear giggling.

"Is this the pool room?" I ask, and open the door without waiting for him to answer.

Inside, the Glitches, James, and John are in an inflatable gray pool that's as tall as a sidewalk curb, sitting in maybe an inch of water. The twins poke the plastic pool with crochet hooks, and the Glitches pat the top of the water, making minuscule splashes, and then curve their arms like they're in a synchronized swimming competition.

They crack their faces in my direction, their gleeful expressions perfectly in sync.

I shut the door and walk away without another word.

Another disturbing thought crosses my mind. Peace. Jacob's brothers. The Glitches. If Eloise were here, she'd fit right in—similar age and features. I can't even hear their music to differentiate between them. Everyone is silent.

They have something else in common too—Dr. Whisper and that spooky clinic. I have to find out how he's treating these kids.

Outside is still hauntingly empty, like an abandoned ghost town. With a few set design changes, this place would be perfect for shooting one of those dramatic cowboy standoff scenes in a Western. Except there's no wind to blow tumbleweeds down the path.

Without thinking, I start to whistle a cowboy tune. Jacob gasps and slaps a hand over my mouth. His fear stops us both in our tracks. The echo of the whistle seems to go on for a whole chorus, and the white lights around the perimeter flicker. After a few seconds, he releases a breath.

"I dunno how you got away with that," he says, looking at me as if I'm the luckiest person in the world. Meanwhile, I feel like a cat with one life remaining.

As we walk across the courtyard, I glance at the house with the blacked-out windows. Now it all makes sense with the bright curtain-penetrating lights from last night, and I wonder if it was Jacob's idea.

"I should paint my windows too," I say, pointing at them. "I barely got any sleep last night."

"I'd stay away from that house if I were you. It creeps me out," he replies with a shudder.

"Sorry?" I glance at him with furrowed eyebrows. "What's inside—"

Jacob puts both hands in the air. "I don't want to know."

There's a flash of guilt on his face. Why would he warn me from a property I saw him enter earlier? What is he hiding?

I chide myself for being so naive, thinking I could trust someone I've barely known for two seconds. And I just declared my intention to break into the clinic; he could rat me out to his dad.

Jacob senses my suspicion. "Maybe Dr. Whisper stores equipment in there."

I nod, but Jacob still seems worried.

"Fun fact. Did you know Bob Marley sang backing vocals for Jackie Opel when he recorded in Jamaica?"

"Yup. So did Peter Tosh." He relaxes his shoulders and then starts to chat about his favorite spouge songs.

I should be more cautious until I find out what he's hiding, but for now, I don't have a choice but to confide in him. I can worry about him after I find my parents and learn what's happening to Peace.

As we get closer to the structure with the stale corn smell, there is a loud clink, maybe just over the sound limit. The lights flicker again. Jacob gestures ahead with the mop, and we rush up the steps.

Immediately there's an assault on all my senses. The smell of stale corn amplified by one hundred. There's a slight rustling in the air, as if a room of people got attacked by a swarm of sandflies and they were scratching at the same time. My eyes adjust to the low light and follow the rows of cages stacked along the walls, from the floor to the ceiling. I start scanning the room for the key card.

"Hey, Dad," he calls. "We're here to help clean up." In a darker corner of the room, Uncle Newton waves at us with the hammer in his hand and a nail in his mouth.

"You're just in time to witness the finale. It's gonna be rad," he says in a muffled voice, fiddling with a cage.

I can't decide if I'm more scared by the thought of him accidentally swallowing that nail or the fact that I'd have to find Dr. Whisper to treat him.

"Been waiting to fix this latch for the last week," he says, moving the nail to the side of his mouth with his teeth. "Just seven more hits and it's done." He grips the door and stares at the large watch on his hand.

"Why'd it take so long to fix a latch?" I ask.

Uncle Newton scoffs and then coughs. Jacob rushes to help before he has a nail for breakfast.

"I got special permission to give it a good hit for the next thirty minutes today," he says, removing the nail from his mouth. He hits the nail with the tiniest of taps, before giving it a whack with the hammer. About sixty decibels. Breaching the sound limit. No wonder a five-minute job took over a week to finish.

"Selena, can you go ahead and feed the rabbits?" Uncle Newton says, and points at a bowl of brown pellets on a table.

"Serenity."

"Yes, very peaceful today."

Jacob and I roll our eyes at the same time, but I get the bowl, happy for an excuse to rove around the hut for the key card.

I peer into the closest cage. There's a furry carpet, a ceramic swan-shaped bowl of water, and knitted trees with yarn carrots hanging from the branches—made by Jacob's brothers, I assume. It's a five-star rabbit cage, that's for sure.

"Here, bunny bunny," I murmur, poking an extra-long pellet through a hole. There's movement at the back of the cage, and suddenly two large red eyes appear in the dark. "Come and get it."

The rabbit comes into the light, and I yank my finger out of the cage.

It is completely hairless, with spots around its eyes like heart-shaped sunglasses. It resembles a pink wrinkled balloon with long ears. It twitches its nose, sniffing for the meal, but I'm afraid to open the latch in case it thinks my face looks delicious. I glance over at Jacob and Uncle Newton, but they're focused on fixing the cage.

I take a deep breath and remind myself that I'm a filmmaker who traveled to a haunted island and trekked through the forest alone. There's nothing scary about a timid little bunny.

I undo the latch and reach into the cage with a handful of pellets. The rabbit takes a tiny hop forward and opens its mouth to reveal a humongous curved front tooth, ready to clamp down on my fingers.

I gasp and scream at the same time, the result being a choking gurgle. I fling the food away and my hand bangs into the cage.

The rabbit spasms and leaps into the air. It crashes into

the top of the cage, and there is a sickening crunch and an even more distressing thud as it lands on the carpet.

Lifeless. As still as a stuffed toy.

"Oh no, not Timoteeth," Uncle Newton moans.

When I glance across at the other cages, all the other hairless rabbits are pressed against the cage doors, as if straining to see what happened.

Then they all turn to me and start to stomp on the bottom of their cages, and though the sound is mellowed by the carpet, the soft thuds remind me of the stampeding score from *Jumanji* movies, just before the animals crash through the house.

I panic and back away from the cage, but I can't stop staring at the rabbits, their red eyes on me and mouths open in quiet screams.

TAKE 16—*ANIMA MONTIUM*

There is a scene in a zombie film where the last survivor is pressed against a wrecked car, with no means of defense, and the slow march of death comes closer and closer.

That's how I feel here in the hut, with all those rabbits stomping in their cages. Except in my case, I am the flesh-eating zombie—I'm the one who invaded their space and brought death.

Uncle Newton hurries over to the cage, for the first time without a smile on his face. The transformation is remarkable, from a jester to a strict teacher. I imagine his music would sound like a snapping pencil.

"I—I—I didn't mean— I'm sorry— I—" But I don't know what to say.

Uncle Newton opens the cage and gently strokes Timoteeth along his twisted back. His nose makes a small twitch and I buckle against the table with relief. He's alive.

Jacob exhales. "I'm beginning to think you're bad luck."

"It's okay, just a little fracture," Uncle Newton murmurs.

I force myself to look at his face, and to my surprise he's smiling. Jovial Uncle Newton has returned.

A fracture? I'm no doctor, but even I know that a rabbit shouldn't look like a horseshoe. I sink to the floor with tears in my eyes.

"Dear, dear Serena." Uncle Newton pats me on top of my head. "Let's go to the clinic. Dr. Whisper will fix him right up."

The mention of Dr. Whisper is enough to cause all my tears to dry up. He's going to fix me too. After our encounter this morning, I'm already treading a thin line today.

At that moment, all the rabbits stop stomping in their cages. It must be a coincidence; rabbits can't recognize names . . . can they?

Uncle Newton pats his pants pockets. "Now where did I put that pass? Oh, right." He pulls a gray key card from an empty water bowl. Then he scoops Timoteeth up in his hands and cradles him like a baby.

I keep my face down as I follow them outside, still feeling the red glares from the rabbits.

I only raise my head when we're in front of the clinic. My reflection in the mirrored doors looks pitiful and unbalanced without my headphones.

This isn't how I planned to get into the clinic, but I shove aside my guilt. I need to investigate inside the building.

Uncle Newton opens a metal box at the side of the door

and reveals a shiny black panel. He waves the pass in front of it and a red dot blinks twice.

Then there are two small beeps, like a bird's chirp.

And just like that, my mind vaults into my nightmare. It looks like the panel in the corridor, except it's missing the NO ENTRY sign.

Then the door opens with a soft hiss—one I'd recognize anywhere.

My heart beats fast and loud in my ears. So loud I'm surprised the sound meters don't pick it up. My iPod is charging in the house, but that doesn't stop me from scratching at my pocket, hoping the device will somehow sense my panic and make its way to me. Uncle Newton and Jacob step inside and wait for me to follow, but my feet are rooted to the spot.

A flicker of confusion comes across Jacob's face.

I swallow the bubble of fear in my throat. "I'm not. Dr. Whisper, um, he— I can't."

"Don't worry, we'll take care of everything," Uncle Newton reassures me. My throat is so dry, I can't say a word.

Though I can't bring my feet to move, I lean forward to get a glimpse inside.

Stark white walls. Gleaming interior. There is a large poster on the wall, a collage of happy families. A mother and father chasing after a child in a sunflower field, two mothers cuddling a baby in a cradle, a father smiling up at a gleeful baby he's tossed into the air. A banner with the text YOUR

PERFECT CHILD in white bold letters. The last thing I notice before the doors close is a gray couch in the corner.

There's no way this is the building from my nightmare. This is not the building from my nightmare. There are millions of gray couches in the world. This is not the building from—but why does it seem so familiar?

I take a shaky step closer to the black panel. The red light is gone, leaving the tiny circle as gray as the clouds. For some reason, I reach out a hand to touch it.

"Serenity."

My hand freezes, the breath caught in my throat. I gaze in the reflection in the doors, but there's no one around. I take a step back.

"Serenity."

This time I scurry away from the door. It sounds like my mother! She seems near yet far away, like she's calling from underground. My hands tremble as I peer at the gray tiles, thinking about my parents calling me from a grave. Maybe I *am* watching too many horror movies.

"Mum?" I look around the courtyard again.

"Serenity."

This time, the voice seems to come from behind the clinic. I dart through the small space between the rabbit hut and the clinic, relief rushing through my body.

But the space is empty.

"Mum?" I call again, but there's no reply. Could it be that

I'm so desperate to find my parents, I'm hearing their voices in the trees?

I walk over to the edge of the fence, the same place I climbed to enter the facility. Yesterday I was too intimidated by the building to notice the subtle view of the sea in the distance.

I press against the fence and look down. The clinic is much bigger than I realized, with multiple stories built down the side of the cliff. It seems bigger than my local cinema, which can easily hold an audience of four hundred people.

The wired fencing stops just before the edge of the jagged rocks, as if they wanted to prevent anyone from leaping off, and trails along the edge until it reaches the border of the forest.

Dead brown leaves hang from dark branches in disappointment. The branches tangle around one another, growing in all directions, seeming like they would attack anyone who tried to make it through. The foliage pushes against the fence, threatening to break it down.

"Serenity."

It's Mum again, this time louder. Actually, louder than I've ever heard her. She sounds so melodic, so full of life. There was music in her voice; not just the pitter of rain, but how sunshine would sound if it could sing.

Mum seems to be near the thickest part of the bushes, where the leaves intertwine with one another in tight knots.

This must be a mistake. Why would she be in a forbidden forest? I move closer to the edge, and part of a branch stands out from the rest because it shimmers so brightly I have to put a hand above my eyes.

There's still no sign of Mum, but then the circle of light moves and flutters up onto a higher branch.

It's the silver butterfly! I can't help but gasp at the fluorescent colors under its wings.

This time I don't run. All the initial shock and fear has been replaced by curiosity.

The butterfly's twinkling music intensifies as it flutters into the air, along with something else.

Some kind of light staccato tune. The cowboy whistle?

I move closer to the butterfly, closer to the fence. I want to rush over, but I'm afraid to scare it away. Dr. Whisper was wrong . . . or lying. The silver butterfly, the *Anima montium*, is as extinct as humans on Duppy Island.

And I have no proof; no one will believe the word of a twelve-year-old filmmaker. If only I had my phone or my camera . . . Maybe I can catch it in my hands.

At that moment, the butterfly disappears into the thick brush. I rush toward the area, fully intending to climb the fence and follow it into the trees. The dry brown grass gives a satisfying crunch as my sneakers crush it into the ground.

"Serenity!"

The forceful whisper comes from behind. I swirl to see

my parents by the clinic, wearing gray tunics and faces full of outrage.

I immediately forget about the butterfly as waves of relief wash over me. They're not gagged or buried alive or injured in any way. I start to sprint toward them with my arms outstretched but then remember they've avoided me since I arrived. I slow my pace and trudge toward them with a vexed face; it won't be a happy reunion.

As I get nearer, the doors open and Uncle Newton exits with a cage in his hands. He beams at me and points to the rabbit in the cage. Jacob eases out of the clinic behind him and gapes at my parents and then at the bunny in fascinated horror.

Timoteeth is nibbling on a blade of grass that looks too green to be real and happily leaping around the cage.

TAKE 17—IT WASN'T ME

My parents are so mad they don't give me a chance to answer their whisper-questions.

"What are you doing here?" "What were you thinking?" and "Gran must be so worried!" all merge together into a chorus of disapproval, and all the while I'm staring, open-mouthed, at the beaming Uncle Newton and the fully healed bunny hopping about the cage.

For the second time today, I'm left speechless. I can't believe it's the same rabbit, but the heart-shaped spots around the eyes confirm Timoteeth's identity. How is this possible?

Jacob sticks a finger in the cage and Timoteeth gets up on his hind legs and nudges it lovingly with his nose. Jacob gives me his "I don't want to know" face, and I remember that I can't trust him either.

"Serenity, we're speaking to you." There's no cheerful music in Mum's voice for sure. The previous calls had to be cruel tricks of the wind.

Mum folds her arms and gives me a stern look. But I'm not the only guilty party here.

I cross my arms as well. "So when are we going to talk about you two lying and hightailing it to a creepy island so Peace can get some kind of zombie treatment?"

Mum lets out a tiny gasp, and her eyes dart to Uncle Newton and Jacob. There's a long, long, long sigh from Dad.

Uncle Newton clears his throat. "Come along, son. I need help fixing the cage before time runs out."

Dad waits until they are out of earshot. "Look, Serenity, we didn't want you to worry. Peace is fine, we promise."

"He's not 'fine.' Haven't you noticed how he's changed?"

"Changed? In what way?" Mum asks, concerned.

I gawk at my parents, and as I stare I notice they look . . . refreshed. The dark circles under their eyes are gone. No puffiness and their skin is glowing. It's like they've been resting for two months, not two days. I guess this is what happens when they get a break from me.

"Have you been in these sessions with Peace and Dr. Whisper?" I ask, trying to hide the hurt.

"A few," Dad replies.

"Well, you didn't see him last night. He was so out of it."

To my surprise, wide smiles come across their faces. "We know. Peace finally slept through the night. He was as still as a stuffed bear," Dad chirps.

I'm so confused. Did my parents sneak into Peace's

bedroom after I fell asleep yesterday and leave before I woke up?

"No, I mean he's different—not in a good way!" I reply, struggling to keep calm. "He's not fine. Not fine at all."

"You're right." Mum shares this knowing look with Dad. "Peace is more than fine. These are his last sessions. In fact, Dr. Whisper says we can leave in another week, instead of staying till month end."

"But you're still heading home when the boat returns on Friday, young lady." Dad wags a finger in my face. "And you're grounded, indefinitely."

I'm too worked up to care. How can they not see the ruthless change in Peace? I point to Timoteeth's cage before Uncle Newton disappears between the space.

"You see that rabbit? Its back was broken not even ten minutes ago. Whatever treatment Dr. Whisper is carrying out in there isn't normal."

Mum dismisses me with her hand. "Serenity, it's just some counseling to help with his fear of the dark—nothing more than that."

I throw my arms in the air. "So why do all the kids here act like they're being drugged and—"

Mum shushes me before I can finish. "Serenity, he's already made significant progress with your brother. Dr. Whisper is highly respected and very understanding."

"Oh, really? So why is he forcing me to be a maid?"

Mum tuts. "Stop exaggerating; everyone here has to do chores. I want you to be on your best behavior for the next two days."

It's the perfect moment, too perfect, for a scowling Dr. Whisper to step out of the clinic with Peace, who has a canvas in his hands and tears streaming down his cheeks.

Peace flips the canvas and reveals jagged slashes of red paint all over the white painting. His bottom lip trembles as he points at me. "Look what she did."

Picture that moment in a movie when an amateur detective finds a mangled body on the floor. They notice a bloody knife in the corner, and against all reason, pick it up just in time for a nosy neighbor to see them standing over the body with the murder weapon.

That's the look my parents give me when I inexplicably reach out to touch the red slashes on the painting.

Peace twists the canvas away, runs to Mum, and quietly sobs into her hip. But then I notice Peace's sniffles are different—no mewling noises, but sharp intakes like he's struggling to breathe. He turns to me and there is a spiteful smile on his face.

Peace set me up.

I take a deep breath. It's hard to keep your voice calm when you're being framed. "Mum, Dad, it wasn't me."

"I saw you with the paint," Peace whispers with a sniffle. I catch the smug look on his face before he pretends to cry again.

"I didn't do this." I grab Dad's hand, pleading. "I was with Jacob the entire time, I swear."

"The Newtons were in here with me, occupied with an injured animal." Dr. Whisper tilts his head. "You seem to like . . . breaking things."

My heart skips a beat, but I continue to defend myself, pointing to the trees with a trembling finger. "But I—I—I wasn't in the common room. I was over there looking at the silver butterfly."

Dr. Whisper grinds his teeth. "That is very hard to believe since, as I told you, the *Anima montium* is extinct."

"*Anima*? What's that about a soul?" asks Dad, interested now that a Latin word has entered the conversation.

"No, it's not! I saw the silver butterfly! If I had my camera, I could shoot footage for a documentary—"

Mum claps twice, harder than I've heard her. "Enough. You and I both know you're not interested in documentaries."

Dr. Whisper shoots me a dark look. "Mr. and Mrs. Noah, I'm afraid your daughter has been a nuisance since she arrived. Rude, disruptive, and has clear contempt for rules. If she continues to be troublesome, I'll have to make immediate arrangements for her departure."

My parents don't seem annoyed anymore—it's worse. They're looking at me with sadness, fatigue, and worry. Now that I can't hear their score, they seem more distant than ever.

Peace pretends to wipe away tears. "Maybe Dr. Whisper can help her," he says in a whiny, childish tone I've never heard before.

The hairs on my arms stand on end, and for a moment, I cannot speak. Peace has turned into a cruel, horrid little person after spending two days here. I don't know what Dr. Whisper's done to my brother, but I'm not letting him give me the same treatment.

Dad sighs. "We simply can't afford it."

"You—we're not rich?" Peace is so stunned he forgot to keep the sniffles in his voice.

"No, son," Dad replies patiently.

"What if I want a new toy? Or to go to Disney World? Can we even afford a pony?" he asks in a quivering voice.

We all give him puzzled looks; Peace has never asked for anything, much less cared about money. Mum lowers her head, and in this silence, you can almost hear her heart breaking. Dad goes next to her and puts an arm around her waist.

"Peace, you're too young to worry about these things. Once you have food, shelter, and a loving family, you're better off than most."

Mum forces a smile, but she awkwardly twists her hands. There's something more going on here.

"Dr. Whisper is rich," Peace mutters under his breath. No one else hears but me.

Dr. Whisper shoots me another spiteful glare. "I believe you have chores to finish." He waves his hand over the panel and steps inside the sliding doors. "I will be in my office when everyone is ready."

I get a glimpse of a long, empty hallway before the doors close behind him. I've been in plenty of white gleaming spaces—the dentist, the computer store, posh clothing shops—but there's something about this building that disturbs me. I know this place—my heart tells me it's familiar even when my brain urges me to forget.

"At least apologize to your brother," Mum says in a tired voice.

I fold my lips. I will not confess to a crime I did not commit.

"Serenity should be punished." Peace reaches into his pocket, pulls out my iPod and headphones, and gives them to my parents.

I can't believe Peace would stoop so low. "No, please, not my music!"

My parents seem confused. I pray they realize something is wrong; my brother would never be so vengeful.

"Sorry, kid," Dad says, resting a hand on my shoulder. "You ruined something precious to Peace. It's only fair."

But Mum sees my distraught face and takes pity on me. "We'll return your iPod if you behave yourself and keep out of trouble."

She pulls one of the gray key cards from her pocket and they head to the clinic doors. Peace shoots me a gloating look that makes his message clear:

You don't belong.

My blood begins to boil, so hot it feels like my head is about to explode. No one believes I saw the silver butterfly! I wish I could expose the real liars—Dr. Whisper and Peace. If I can find evidence, my parents will *have* to believe me. They'll finally agree there's something wrong with Peace. They'll realize Dr. Whisper is a fraud who needs to be exposed, before he and his "treatments" do long-lasting damage to my brother.

"Psst!"

Jacob beckons to me from the space between the wall and the warren.

I hurry over and squeeze in next to him. "What happened in there? You left with a broken rabbit, and a few minutes later he's totally fixed."

"I didn't go in the lab, so I'm just as shocked as you," he replies. But I don't know whether to believe him. "The sooner you learn to stop asking questions here, the better."

"And why didn't you go in the lab?" I jab my finger at his chest.

"And why didn't you come into the clinic?" He jabs a finger right back at me.

I pause, not wanting to confess about my nightmare. "I

decided it was best not to break any more rules," I lie.

He gives a snort of laughter. "How ironic. As soon as you start following the rules, I break one of them."

Jacob lifts up his shirt and pulls my camera from his waistband. I almost scream with joy. I grab my camera and give it a tight hug. "It was in the reception desk, top drawer, wasn't even locked. Now we can shoot our film!"

Now I can prove the silver butterfly exists!

"You are amazing," I say, and I actually mean it. Jacob flushes with embarrassment, and I become aware that we're close together in a small space. I step away and pretend there's something interesting in the sky.

"See, everything worked out. You found your parents and they're fine. Peace is just probably in a bad mood."

I don't respond. Instead I check the camera to make sure it still has a charge.

"I have to help Newton, but you can start on the grass and I'll join you as soon as I can. Hopefully we'll finish in time to shoot a few scenes?"

I nod and pretend to be excited about zombies. This must be the first time I'm more interested in nature than monsters. I follow Jacob to the courtyard, but when he disappears in the warren, I double back through the small space.

I take a quick glance around and then rush to the end of the fence. If I get caught sneaking into the forest, Dr.

Whisper will put me on the next plane out of here on my parents' dime, but I have to take the risk. For Peace.

With everyone out of the way for at least a half hour, it's the perfect time to go on a quick butterfly hunt . . . and a good filmmaker always gets their shot.

TAKE 18—THE FACELESS

I scale the fence and head to the area where I last saw the butterfly, my camera ready to capture any sudden movements.

I crawl through the small path in the bushes, admiring the uncoordinated greens and the way the vines intertwine.

A giggle bubbles in my throat. There's something thrilling about risking the wrath of my family to capture the truth.

Then I hear music. It's soft, but if you listen carefully, you can hear the breeze dancing through branches, raindrops dripping off leaves, and water sliding off stones—the melody of nature.

The ground gets softer and softer and more alive as I push through, and soon there's no need to push at all. Though it's early afternoon, there's a lingering fog in the forest, similar to a candle just after it's blown out. It creates a smoky intrigue, with air that looks chilly but feels like warm breath.

I find myself in the circle of tall coconut trees and capture an amazing wide shot of leaves fanning across the sky. My mouth waters at the thought of fresh coconut water.

The music of the plants and trees is so commanding, I can't help but hum along. And there's no one to shush me! How is it that this foggy, damp forest is my happy place, even without my iPod?

I spot a green caterpillar munching on a leaf, just above tree bark with pointed thorns that look painful to touch. Finally! Some kind of life. I zoom in on the caterpillar and notice a flicker of light at the bottom of the frame.

The silver butterfly!

By the time I zoom out, the light is gone, disappearing between some vines.

Cue the fast-paced drumbeat as I follow the spot of silver light through the trees while trying to avoid tripping on the thickening vines on the forest floor.

The music is getting stronger, not with birds or crickets, but it's as though the butterfly is raising its melody. I can hear its dainty grace in the wind.

"Come on, just one shot," I mumble as the butterfly pauses on a leaf. It flaps its wings and shows off the crescent-shaped circles on the underside. I'm so close to recording history, and even better, proving my parents wrong. But I miss the shot because the camera was out of focus, and it flies away before I can capture a clean one.

The trees open up into a second clearing, this one almost four times the size of the coconut tree clearing beyond the fence. Around the border are dozens of Bajan cherry trees, with the small red cherries growing in thick bunches. They look like tiny sweet peppers, and the ground is littered with their flat, chewy seeds. I've never had such a yearning for fresh fruit.

The cherry trees seem to transform the loud music of the forest into a soft hum, like the choir does in a church while the pastor is preaching.

In the middle of the clearing, on a large mound of dirt the size of a bathtub, are hundreds of silver butterflies, flapping their wings in soundless applause.

My mouth drops open in awe as I get closer to the flutter of butterflies, moving along the soil like gentle waves in the sea. I stop a few feet away, still far enough to not scare them into flight, but close enough to see them huddled around the mound. They flap their wings as if showing off for the camera.

I crouch, lift my camera to my eyes, and press record. I'll probably get chided for breaking the rules, but this is so worth it for my "I told you so" moment and also my future *The Silver Butterfly Lives* documentary.

The soil gives a slight shiver, and though the butterflies move in a ripple, they don't fly away. Alarm bells go off in my head, but I ignore them, keeping my camera trained on the butterflies in anticipation.

The mound shakes again, and I take a step back and zoom out, preparing for the wide shot. Then the mound of dirt stands up, and soil falls off a skinny body that would be my height if not for a pointy mushroom hat on its head.

I move the camera away from my face and fall onto my bottom, staring at the sight before me. The butterflies don't take flight and instead cover the body like a cloth, nesting in the coconut-palm skirt around its waist.

It's a boy! Why is he hiding in dirt?

"Hello?" I croak, and then clear my throat. "Are you okay?"

He doesn't respond. I get to my feet, the camera still recording in my hands. I know I should go closer to see if he's hurt, but I'm frozen to the spot.

Then the boy lifts his head.

His face is as empty as Peace's canvas. He has no eyes or nose, nothing except two lips as thin as earthworms. The sight sends chills all the way into the insides of my bones.

It's a douen.

A faceless child.

The actual creature in the flesh is a hundred times scarier than the illustration from the internet. Skin caked in mud. A sharp stench of rotting fruit. And though it has no eyes, I can *feel* its stare, as intense as a snake about to strike.

Its tummy seems bloated, with a protruding lump in the center, as if it swallowed something too big for its belly to digest. The lump shifts downward, disrupting a few butterflies from the coconut-palm skirt.

Blood rushes through my veins, and suddenly I'm not cold anymore. But my heart races faster than a galloping horse and it hurts to breathe. This is it. This is what has been haunting me for my whole life. I couldn't remember the face of the monster behind the door in my nightmare because *it does not have one.*

The douen slowly pulls its feet from the mound, rounded heels coming out first and then its toes, pointed in the opposite direction. It takes a step forward and seems to glide toward me on its backward feet. Its twisted footsteps make haunting crunches through the leaves as it gets closer. It slowly cocks its head to one side side and extends a bony, muddy hand. Calling me. Begging me to join it. If this douen gets a hold of me, it may never let go.

My brain screams at my legs to run, but they've forgotten their function. The camera falls from my limp fingers and lands on the grass with a soft thud.

The douen brushes some dirt away from his upper-right cheek, revealing a moon-shaped dark mark on his brown skin. It forms its mouth into a perfectly round circle the size of a cherry and lets out a whistle.

My cowboy whistle.

And that's what it takes for my legs to remember how to work, and for the howling cry building up in my brain to leave my mouth.

I dash through the forest, not knowing if the path leads back to the facility, my scream echoing in the trees.

TAKE 19—LOCKED UP

There should be close-up shots of my face in terror.

Quick cuts of my body slamming into trees and vines clinging to me like bony fingers. Heavy breathing. Show my sneakers sliding in mud and hands scraping against sharp rocks. Yet every way I turn, there is a creature with no face, mouth open and beckoning for me to follow.

I stop trying to remember the path and run by instinct, squirming through thick bushes, my nails ripping away the leaves. My gut tells me to move away from music, so that's what I do, even as my brain screams for me to follow the rhythm.

Suddenly I hit a fence. I pull some vines away and cry out with relief at the sight of the bathrooms on the facility. Behind me, an echo whispers my name, and sharp nails tug at my shirt. I yelp and scramble up the fence faster than a lizard on fire.

The sound meters start to spin as I get close to the top. Then the bright lights on the facility's roof snap on, this time flashing like bolts of lightning. But I don't stop, not even when the rusty metal spikes rip away my jeans.

I hurtle over the top, leaving some of my skin behind on the spikes. My body makes the loudest thud into the marl and knocks the wind out of my chest, but I don't have time to recover.

I dash toward our house, shouting for my parents, but when I get near the bathrooms, something sharp jabs me in the back.

The creature is trying to rip my heart out from behind!

I let out another bloodcurdling cry and take a swing but trip over something small and solid. It scratches at my throat, and I scramble off the douen while bawling for my parents. I want to keep quiet, but my mind won't let me. My throat is on fire; I want my parents; I want to go home.

Without a sound, the douen dashes across the courtyard with lightning speed toward the clinic. As if the building saw it coming, metal doors slide down over the glass entrance. Then something grabs me from behind.

"Serenity!" Another hushed but urgent whisper. I squeeze my eyes shut, not wanting to look, and my scream escalates, but a hand claps itself over my mouth.

"Please, please, please stop." I recognize the voice through my terror and open my eyes. It's Jacob, looking more sickly than ever, and we're surrounded by flashing red lights.

"I saw a douen," I gasp, clutching onto his shoulders. I

point toward the courtyard, where Uncle Newton races after the creature with a hammer.

Jacob's eyes widen, and he sways on the spot before joining me on the ground. I find the strength to sit up, trying to regain my breath, but I nearly start screaming again when I glance to the right of the courtyard.

The Glitches, now in damp leotards, are spasming around the space in a circle, with their hands clapped over their ears and eyes rolled back in their heads. They look like they're short-circuiting, and even in my horror, I wish that I had a camera to record, because they actually look like break-dancing zombies.

One of Jacob's brothers stumbles toward us with a crochet hook in his hand. His eyes are stark white and laced with bloodshot veins.

I scurry away but Jacob races to him. "John? James! What's wrong with you?!" he cries. I hope he doesn't gut Jacob with the hook.

Suddenly there's a loud click, and all the lights stop flashing. After a moment of complete stillness, the Glitches collapse onto the ground. Their pupils return to their eyeballs and they stare straight ahead with blank expressions. John (or James) flops into Jacob's arms like a wet noodle.

The metal door slides up with a clink, and the glass doors open.

Out steps Dr. Whisper, his face so thunderous that the

bulging veins look like vines snaking over his skin. As he strides across the courtyard, fear gnaws at my gut, urging me to run. But where? I'm trapped here, stuck between a faceless douen and a two-faced doctor.

Dr. Whisper steps over the Glitches as if they were human-sized potholes. Jacob backs away from him, still struggling to prop up James (or John) in his arms. There's no sign of my parents or Uncle Newton. We're alone to face his wrath.

"One day," he says in his cold voice. "One day to set off the alarms."

He glances at Jacob. "And I know she did it. Don't try to cover for her again."

Jacob averts his eyes and gently lays his brother on the ground.

"Douens!" I cry out, and Dr. Whisper flinches. I try again in my whisper voice. "Douens, here on the compound."

"Don't be ridiculous. Are you always so obsessed with things that do not exist?"

"I'm serious, Uncle Newton went after it!"

"Serenity," Jacob says solemnly. "That wasn't a douen. My brothers tried to prank you, but they weren't counting on your reaction. John got scared and ran away."

He points at a silver crochet hook on the ground.

"No, but, but—" I stumble on my words, thinking about if I actually saw a face. "It followed me, from the forest."

Both Jacob and Dr. Whisper gasp. It's the first time I've

seen fear on Dr. Whisper's face. It looks strangely out of place.

"How could you be so foolish," Dr. Whisper says, his voice shaking. "You've put us all in danger."

The Glitches start moving on the ground, moaning and holding their heads. But as soon as they set sight on Dr. Whisper, the light comes back into their eyes and they try to get to their feet and bow at the same time.

Uncle Newton approaches us with an apologetic expression. "I must not know my own strength," he says, lifting the hammer in the air. "I didn't mean to set off the alarm."

James whimpers and sits up, reaching for Uncle Newton, who lifts him to his feet and presses a hand against his forehead. "John, you're burning up."

"That's James, Newton. Did you catch John?" Jacob says, his face bent with concern.

Uncle Newton seems confused. "John?"

Hope sparks in my chest. Maybe it was a douen after all. Then everyone will have to believe me.

"Oh, John!" Uncle Newton says with a chuckle. "I'm sure he's around somewhere. Chillax!"

Jacob and I exchange horrified glances. Nothing makes sense right now. Why would the Glitches react like this to a little noise? And we both saw Uncle Newton chasing after John. How can he pretend that everything is okay? And where is my family?!

A strong hand grips my arm.

"I've been waiting to do this since you got here." Dr. Whisper pulls me across the grass, and it's hard to keep up with his long strides. As I stumble behind him, I glance over my shoulder and notice Jacob, staring after us and biting his nails.

We're headed to the chattel house with the blacked-out windows.

I try to twist my hand away, but his grip is too tight.

When we step inside, my eyes have to adjust to the darkness. I expect it to be dusty or have a moldy smell, but there's a sweet tanginess in the air. Dr. Whisper switches on a pen light, walks to the middle of the room, and lifts up a hatch.

It sounds like a rake being dragged across cement—a terrible, slow *scrrrriitttttch*.

"Please, I'm sorry," I beg. "I won't break the rules ever again." But Dr. Whisper forces me to follow him down some stairs.

As we get close to the bottom, there's a grating sound in the air, like dull scissors fighting to cut through a clump of hair. I'm so scared my knees start to get weak, and I clutch on to his coat. I expect him to push me away, but Dr. Whisper smirks, his gleaming white teeth eating away some of the darkness.

Inside, the cellar smells of mold and earth, and the sound gets stronger and stronger. Dr. Whisper removes the watch from my wrist, pries my hand off his coat, and pushes me into a space.

He slides bars across and a lock clicks. Real-life rusty bars. A prison cell under the chattel house.

"Don't ever accuse me of being inconsiderate," he says. "You can finally be as loud as you want down here. No one can hear you scream."

That doesn't stop me from trying. I holler as loud as I can. I shake the bars but stop when dirt falls from the roof. I don't trust that the house won't collapse and bury me alive. I hum and pace around the cell, singing "The Ants Go Marching" over and over again, but it doesn't help.

I don't know how much time has passed; I don't know if my parents know where I am, or worse, if they're aware and aren't coming to save me. I squeeze myself into the smallest corner of the cell, rocking on the ground, and then I hear it.

A faint whistle.

I press my ear to the dirty wall and recognize the cowboy tune. I become so scared I get numb, unable to feel my hands or my feet. Suppose this is similar to a lion's den?

A douen's den.

After the whistle, the bars will slide open, and douens will close in on me, stalking their prey. Maybe they like to play with their food before they eat it? I'll soon be the lump trying to escape a douen's belly. I have no place to hide and no way to fight them.

But then the whistle changes to a cheerful tune, like a bird's melody to chicks in a nest. Eventually, after no douens burst into the cell, my fears melt away.

If I were to score this scene, I'd make that lullaby tune echo throughout the cellar, even though it's as faint as a breath. Because the audience has to understand how, on the hard floor in a dirty cell, I was able to eventually fall asleep.

TAKE 20—ONE OF US IS MISSING

The silence wakes me up. I've never really understood the expression "time stood still" until now. My right knee throbs and the sweat stings where it runs across the various scrapes and scratches on my body.

"Hello?" I whisper, and place my hand on the wall. The whistling was the only thing that kept me grounded; it was a shining light of hope.

Suddenly there's an actual shining light. Followed by the roar of pouring rain and the faint sound of a trapped bird fluttering in a cage.

"Trinity! What are you doing down here in the dark?"

A beam floods the cell and I hide my face behind my arm. It's covered in dried mud and bits of dead leaves; in the darkness you couldn't tell the difference between me and a douen.

"You better unlock this cell right now, Newton!"

"Mum?" I crawl to my feet. The bars rattle, and then a hand slams against them.

No wonder I didn't recognize Mum's music; it's so loud it overpowers Dad's patter, but I've never been more glad to hear them.

Mum bursts into the cell and lifts me up in her arms, mud and all, and squeezes me in a tight hug. I'm lost in a cloud of mango and mint oil, and all the pain inside fades away.

Dad inspects my face with gentle fingers. His expression is stoic but I can tell he is seething. "Mr. Newton, get us out of here."

"One second, I'm looking for something." Uncle Newton strides around the cell like he's browsing a department store. His beam illuminates a broken, rusty toilet, a faucet, pieces of ceramic and pipe. "If only I could remember what it is," he mumbles. "Ah well!"

He shines the light on me. "You may want to change before the movie starts."

Dad lifts me in his arms. As we climb the stairs, their music starts to fade away. I bury my face in Dad's neck, hoping to hear him for a bit longer.

"Why are there cells down here anyway?" Mum grunts in disgust.

"There was a prison here," he explains. "It became a quarantine facility in 1854 for advanced cholera cases."

"I can't believe Dr. Whisper though. What kind of

time-out is this? I want off this island. I need our phones back right now. We're calling the police." Mum's voice is laced with anger.

Dad sighs. "I'm with you, Naamah, but let's get all the facts first. We'd need to charter a plane and, you know."

I lift my head. "No, no, we need to leave now. Douens."

"It's okay, baby." Mum strokes my face. "These horrors are finally getting to her," she says to Dad.

"No, I saw——"

I stop talking when Uncle Newton opens the door. The blinding lights are so strong it's like pepper in my eyeballs.

"I found your friend!" Uncle Newton chirps.

I crack open an eye and see Jacob next to a bored-looking Peace.

"Newton, we're looking for John. John!" Jacob blows out steam. "Dad, what's the matter with you?"

A flicker of confusion flashes across Uncle Newton's face, but then he brightens again. "Oh right, I'm sure he's around here somewhere."

He struts away, with Jacob whisper-arguing behind him.

"Can we have dinner now?" Peace asks.

Mum looks at him, for once, not with gooey eyes. "Not just yet; we need to have a talk with Dr. Whisper."

My parents won't believe I saw a douen in the forest, and it's not wise to reveal I broke another rule now that they're finally in my corner. But I need answers; seeing the douen opened a door to questions in my brain that had been locked for a long time.

"Have I been to this island before?" I ask.

Their expressions turn from disapproval to shock and then . . . fear?

"So I have been here, then?" I press. "When? And what is Your Perfect Child?"

They stare at each other as though hoping the other will respond first.

"It's complicated," Mum says, looking pained.

It takes all my strength not to yell, but the fuming seemed to work in my favor. For once my parents are more freaked out by my silence than I am.

"It's about time she knew," Dad says with a sigh. Mum clasps her fingers and releases a slow, deep breath.

Then she takes both my hands into hers. "Serenity, there were . . . complications with your birth. We didn't think we could have another baby. We tried so many treatments but none worked . . . until we met Dr. Whisper. I know he's a bit eccentric. But he promised perfection—the perfect child. And then we had Peace."

Mum and Dad exchange a smile. Peace beams as Mum pinches his cheek.

Now it makes sense why they love him more. He's a miracle baby.

"But I still don't understand the treatments."

"The children in the program are supposed to return every year until their sixth birthday for evaluation. Running some tests, making sure everything is fine. We've had, um, some difficulties and only came back this year because of Peace's, um, troubles, and also Dr. Whisper waived his fee," Mum says, unable to meet my eyes.

Peace's face contorts into an ugly grimace. As much as my parents insist he's fine, I know it's not true. His skin has lost its brown shine and seems almost as gray as the sky. And what's so special about age six? Jacob mentioned his brothers were six years old when they started to act out. I wonder how old the Glitches are . . .

Dad continues. "I guess this brings us back to your question. You *have* been here before, when your mum gave birth to Peace. You may have . . . slipped away and caused some damage. It was all my fault. I only left you alone for a second."

Immediate flash to the NO ENTRY sign above the door in my nightmare. I've been haunted by that experience for as long as I can remember. If anything was damaged, it was me.

"I wonder why Dr. Whisper hates me," I mutter.

Dad responds with, "He doesn't hate you" at the same time Mum says, "It's complicated." It's one of those rare moments they're out of sync.

"Come, honey," Mum says, squaring her shoulders. "We need to have a frank talk with Dr. Whisper. In the meantime, you two can start packing."

"Packing?" Peace whirls on the spot. "We can't leave. I'm not done here."

"You heard your mother, son."

Peace shoots a look of loathing at my parents, an expression I have never seen on his face before.

I watch them march toward the clinic like soldiers going off to battle, and when I turn around, Peace is right in front of me, his eyes full of anger. I flinch and take a step back.

"You ruin everything," he hisses. He only reaches my hip, but the size of the hate in his eyes makes him seem so much taller.

Dr. Whisper's treatment may have helped Peace sleep through the night, but now he's a nightmare during the day. Peace needs to get away from that shady doctor—the sooner the better.

I step around him and hurry to the house, still keeping an eye out for douens.

I pull our suitcases from under the bed. Peace can hate me all he wants, but we're getting out of here before my *Face Snatcher* movie comes true. I grab another gray tunic and a pair of jeans and dash to the showers. By the time I make my way back to the house, I feel refreshed, both inside and out.

In the courtyard, Uncle Newton fiddles with a projector on the picnic table, still ignoring Jacob. The Glitches and James are seated in chairs, staring ahead as still as mannequins. When a blue square appears at the side of the clinic, they applaud with their index fingers.

Jacob notices me and I meet him halfway across the grass. I want to unearth as many secrets as I can before I leave.

"What happened?" he asks when I'm in earshot. "Dr. Whisper came out with the biggest smile, so disturbing."

"Why didn't you tell me the house was a prison?" I demand.

Jacob blinks several times. "What?"

"Don't try to deny it. I saw you going in there."

A look of guilt flashes across his face. He checks to make sure no one is listening and then lowers his head. "I'm hiding food, okay?"

"What?"

"Fresh fruit isn't allowed at the facility—believe me, I know," he says at my incredulous expression. "Horace the boatman smuggles in plums for me—those are my favorite. June plums, hog plums, sometimes he brings those preserved Chinese red plums." His eyes grow distant and he licks his lips. It's hard not to believe him when he's about to drool.

"I store them in a coal pot in the corner, and whenever I get a chance, I sneak a bite. I swear, I didn't know anything about a prison down there," he says, forming a cross on his chest. "I just figured you were on a dusty time-out."

Then I remember the faint sweet smell in the air when I first stepped into the house.

"Forgive me?"

"No, because you didn't share," I reply, but I stop glowering at him.

"Did you really go into the forest again?" he asks. I nod, and his face changes from disapproval to alarm as I tell the story. I don't even have to exaggerate; there's no need to create drama when you were chased by douens.

"I *knew* it. It's a miracle you made it back. There's no sign of John, Newton isn't taking his disappearance seriously, and if he's trapped out there with . . ." Jacob's voice trails off.

"My parents are contacting the police," I reassure him. "I'll make sure they report it."

He seems relieved, but then his gaze drifts to the side. I turn to see my parents coming out of the chattel house in formal black dashikis. They beam at me and Jacob, as though they're seeing us for the first time today. Peace steps out from behind them with a smug expression and I get a sinking feeling in my gut.

"Serenity, you missed dinner," Mum scolds with a tut.

"We're watching an animated film tonight! From 1918 Argentina," Dad says, rubbing his hands together with glee. "I don't know how Dr. Whisper does it—there aren't supposed to be any surviving copies of *Sin dejar rastros*."

"B-But, I thought we were going home," I stutter.

"*You* leave on Friday, but we're staying for an extra week. We've been through this already," Mum replies with impatience. I'm baffled by their sudden change in attitude.

I follow them to the gathering, where the Glitches, James, and Uncle Newton are snacking on bowls of marshmallows. I can't shake the dread forming in my chest.

"But you're going to let Dr. Whisper get away with locking me in a prison?"

"Prison? You and your imagination again," Mum laughs, and Dad joins in. Once again, their faces are glowing, their skin so shiny it could have been slathered in olive oil. I gape at them, at a loss for words.

Something happened to my parents while they were in the clinic.

They don't remember.

"Oh, I almost forgot!" Mum cups my cheek. "Dr. Whisper said you did good work today, so we charged your iPod—it's on your dresser. I'm so proud of you."

Then they turn to admire the black-and-white animated video projected on the side of the clinic. Under the bright lights, the images look like watermarks dancing on the wall.

Dr. Whisper steps out of the clinic and our eyes lock. He smirks as I start to back away.

I jump when I sense someone behind me, but it's only

Jacob. He looks as confused and worried as me. "John's missing, and they're all here watching a movie, like nothing's wrong."

My parents throw their heads back in quiet laughter at the film, though there's nothing funny about a sinking ship. Uncle Newton shoves fistfuls of marshmallows into his mouth while James touches the empty seat to his left in confusion.

The Glitches stare at the ground instead of watching the film. An earthworm has stolen their attention. I wrench my gaze away when the Glitches creep after it like a man-made centipede.

"Mum and Dad don't remember," I whisper. Somehow saying it aloud makes it more real. It doesn't seem possible, but Dr. Whisper did more than just change my parents' minds about leaving Duppy Island. He has somehow tampered with their memories.

I tell Jacob my suspicions and watch the many emotions flash across his face. Disbelief. Shock. Doubt. Disbelief again.

"Has your father always been forgetful?" I ask gently.

There's a moment of painful silence, but then words finally come, strained and tense. "Never this bad."

The disturbing truth lingers in the air. Uncle Newton is most likely one of Dr. Whisper's victims too.

Dr. Whisper goes to the empty chair next to James, but Peace stops him and slides over a seat so the doctor can sit between him and my parents. Then Peace looks around and gives me a knowing smile that makes my skin crawl.

I can't depend on my parents to leave the island or keep Dr. Whisper away from Peace. In two days, I'll be sent back home, leaving them all here at Dr. Whisper's mercy.

It's up to me to protect my family, and I'm running out of time to do it.

TAKE 21—BACKWARD

I was expecting my nightmare tonight.

There was a tingling feeling on my skin when I closed my eyes, so powerful the Jackie Opel lyrics seemed to warn me not to fall asleep.

This time, there's no blinding-white room, but a blackness so empty it feels like I'm floating in the night.

Shadows start to twist and coil in the darkness, and then giggle.

I open my mouth to ask what they want, but I have no voice. The more I try to talk, the louder their laughter becomes. My anger turns into tears and my screams run down my face.

Then someone appears behind the shadows. The darkness shifts around a small figure coming toward me. My eyes are drawn to its feet; they are cloven hoofs. Wait—no, not hoofs—cracked heels, with the toes facing the wrong direction. The person's feet are backward.

A douen.

It removes its mushroom hat and a face slides down from its forehead like a wave of sweat.

My dad's face.

"You're so pretty," Dad whispers. "Give me your face." Then, as if the skin flipped a page, the face changes into Mum.

"Let me have your face, darling," she begs in her sweet melodic voice.

A metal door materializes behind me—the one with the NO ENTRY sign. I race toward it and wave my hand across the shiny black panel, but it doesn't open. No red dot, no quiet beeps. I press my ear against the door and hear a sharp cry of pain.

"Help me, please! Ren!"

It's Peace behind the door. I bang on the metal, screaming to be let inside.

"Serenity! Help us!"

My parents are with him! I scratch at the panel until my fingers start to bleed. My family's cries behind the door turn into whimpers and then silence. Then the shadows engulf my body and twist me around.

My eyes fly open and I yank the headphones from my ears. My heart is beating so hard, I press a hand against my chest to keep it inside.

This is it. This is the feeling.

And just like that, I understand, without having to see

what's behind the door. All this time I've been making scary films about monsters, but the real horror isn't zombies, ghouls, or vampires, not even douens.

It's losing people you love.

That's a fear I never want to face.

I take deep breaths, but my heart still thuds in my chest. The nausea is back. I sit up and put my head between my knees. It takes a few minutes, but soon my body begins to relax.

My parents are in the larger bedroom, so tonight is the first time I'm sharing a room with Peace. He avoided my eyes, changed into his pajamas, and slid under his covers without a word. I glance over at his bed in the dim light.

It's empty. Peace probably snuck into my parents' room after I fell asleep.

I toss away the covers and check the time on my watch—I found it next to my fully charged iPod when I dragged Jacob to my room to form a plan.

Duppy Island is dangerous and we need to find a way to call for help. Jacob's normally a stickler for rules, but it didn't take much persuading on my end. First, there was the kid who disappeared, Elijah, and now Jacob's brother is lost in the forest—a forest with faceless children. And if missing kids wasn't enough, an evil doctor is brainwashing our families. Maybe Elijah's parents didn't go looking for him because they forgot he exists . . .

"Let's wait until everyone's asleep and radio the coast guard," I begged Jacob. Who knows what other memories Dr. Whisper could erase after I'm gone?

Jacob shook his head. "Dr. Whisper took the airship's radio after he locked you up."

In the end, we decided to stick with the previous plan: swipe Uncle Newton's key card and sneak into the clinic, find the radio, and inform the coast guard about the missing kids. They'll have to come to the island and investigate.

It's after five a.m. Almost time for sunrise if the island hadn't banned the sun. I pull back the curtains and catch the moment the lights on the clinic's roof power down, going from blinding white to a soft yellow. There's an almost peaceful glow around the facility; even the surrounding trees seem to exhale with relief.

I crack open the door and glance up and down the hallway. My parents' door is closed. When I step out of the bedroom, the rooftop lights flash twice and then disappear.

That's when I hear a noise coming from the kitchen. It takes a second for me to realize it isn't an actual noise but the faint music of a brushstroke.

Peace.

For some reason, I don't call his name. Maybe because I'm afraid to do anything to make his music disappear.

As I sneak to the kitchen, I crouch lower and lower to the ground until I'm practically kissing the floor. Peace is sitting at the dining table but facing the front door, as if he's waiting for someone. I wonder if there's some secret early meeting with Dr. Whisper; maybe I can discover specific details about his treatments.

I duck behind the kitchen counter, folding myself into the space underneath the bar. After a few minutes of silence, I grow restless and have to resist the urge to tap on the tiled floor.

I'm about to give up when Peace walks to the kitchen bar. A spiteful impulse comes over me. He's been so terrible to me over the last few days, he deserves a little scare.

As I reach for Peace's right ankle, he steps away and scratches the foot with his toe. I scowl and reach for his foot again, but both of his feet shift to the right.

And they don't stop.

The bones in his ankles crack as they keep shifting. And turning.

I yank my hand away and cover my mouth to hold in my scream. Peace's feet keep twisting around like a doorknob until they're pointed backward, his shiny cocoa-buttered heels facing the same direction as his kneecaps.

Peace lets out a little sigh of relief and starts to tiptoe to our bedroom. From behind, Peace's toes wriggle in the air, as if they want to crawl up the backs of his legs. He moves like a giant grasshopper. Anyone else would topple forward, but he seems to glide on his backward feet.

Just like the douen in the forest.

Every hair on my skin lifts into the air and a chill sweeps my entire body.

Part of me wants to rush over to Peace to see if he still has a face, but I can't move—it's as if my legs are stuck together.

This is a plot twist out of the scariest horror movie in the world.

My little brother, Peace, is a douen.

TAKE 22—RED LIGHT, GREEN LIGHT

If a gang of flesh-eating bunnies burst through our front door right now, I still wouldn't run into that bedroom with Peace. Instead I curl onto the uncomfortable couch, the wrought iron pressing into my backside, trying to make sense of my discovery.

Has Peace been a douen all along? Sometimes he's so distant it's like I don't know him at all—the silent Peace who stares into space. Is it possible he's been biding his time in the Noah home, waiting for the opportunity to show his true self?

Then I think about the Peace I grew to love. His favorite breakfast is raisin bread with guava jam and a boiled egg. He nods and smiles while you talk, and doesn't interrupt until he's sure you're finished. He gives you a hug just before bed and when he sees you in the morning, even if you're grumpy and still have morning breath.

He's my little brother . . . and my best friend.

No, I would have known if Peace was a douen. It's clear Dr. Whisper is somehow turning him into one now.

But how? And for what purpose? My gut tells me my nightmare about the clinic, the douen behind the metal door, and Dr. Whisper's mysterious treatments are all connected. Not only do I have to break into that clinic to radio for help, but I need to find out how Dr. Whisper is changing Peace.

Mum enters the kitchen, looking radiant in a white-and-gray wrap dress. She stops in her tracks and stares at me, blank-faced. I start to worry Dr. Whisper did permanent damage to her brain, but then she blinks and snaps her fingers.

"Oh, Serenity!" She holds up a pack of instant oatmeal. The "just add water" kind that I hate. "I know you prefer rice porridge, but we don't have any shredded coconut."

I gaze at the towering coconut trees through the window behind her and shake my head in disbelief. It's like dying of thirst during a rainstorm.

Dad steps into the room with a cheerful bounce.

"Why are you in such a good mood this morning?" Mum asks, giving him a peck on the cheek.

I bet Dr. Whisper injected them with some happy potion. I unfold my cramped legs and shake out the stiffness.

"You won't believe it, but I think I found a name. A

popular musician in the 1850s." He sits at the table and taps on his tablet while I try to figure out how to get my clothing from the bedroom without being alone with Peace.

"He may have been my great-great-great-great-great . . ." His voice trails away. I watch as his face goes from confusion to shock and then horror. "Oh no, oh no, please, no."

"It's all gone," Dad groans. "All my files, deleted. All those records."

Mum gasps and grabs the tablet. "What did you do?"

"Nothing! I left my tablet here on the table last night and I—"

They both turn to me at the same time with looks of accusation. I shake my head, but before I can utter a word:

"I told you to leave Dad's tablet alone, Serenity. Why didn't you listen?"

It's Peace. My eyes fly down to his feet. They're facing front again, with no sign of bruising by the ankle. Unfortunately in the time I spend examining his feet, I lose the chance to plead my innocence.

"My notes, all that research," Dad whispers, placing his face in his hands. He looks like he's about to cry.

"I'm sorry, I tried to stop her," Peace says with a small whimper. Mum hurries over to embrace him while glaring at me, and not with the regular anger either. There's real fury in her eyes. She clenches her jaw and marches down the hallway.

They'd never believe me. No one expects Peace to lie.

Mum returns with my iPod and makes a dramatic show of putting it into her pocket. She doesn't have to say a word; the meaning is clear: no more music.

"It's time for meditation," Peace says, and walks out the door with a proud swagger.

Mum gives me the "this isn't over, not by a long shot" look while comforting Dad, who now has his face pressed into the table. I don't know what to do, so I rush outside.

I take my spot next to Jacob, but a few minutes into meditation, I steal a look at Peace and find him gazing at me. There's no more gloating, but I find his emotionless face more disturbing than his other mocking expressions. He shifts his foot and my gaze darts down to his bare toes. They're facing front, as normal.

When I look up, our eyes meet and his face darkens.

He knows.

I close my eyes, but I can still feel his on me. Once, at my old school, a girl shoved me in the back and then laughed when I fell. I complained to Gran and she said, "Duppy know who to frighten." Bullies know who to intimidate and who to leave alone.

Neither of us would ever imagine that one day, Peace would be that bully. But this time, I'm not going to run away from the fight. Not when my brother's life is at stake. There has to be a way to reverse Dr. Whisper's treatments, and I intend to find it.

I'm so engrossed in my thoughts the hour flies by, and when I open my eyes again, Peace is huddled in a closed discussion with the Glitches.

"Our spot, twenty mins," I whisper to Jacob. His gray uniform is rumpled and he looks like he got three minutes of sleep.

"But I haven't found the key—"

"This is an emergency," I reply, before hurrying back to my house to face the rest of my punishment.

Today is Games Day at the facility, and I slip away while Peace, James, and the Glitches play mini golf with balls made of crumpled paper.

I sneak behind the houses to the warren, and as I'm about to duck underneath, I notice a piece of dead earthworm by the bricks. No time to investigate what happened to it.

Jacob is waiting for me, twisting wires on a papier-mâché zombie.

"*Please* tell me everything you know about douens," I say, sitting beside him.

His reaction is as expected: the same grimace I give whenever it's time for family meditation.

"Look, once we stay away from the forest, we're safe . . . at least from the douens." He gives a small chuckle, but the laughter doesn't reach his eyes.

"I've been thinking . . . maybe you saw Elijah. The kid

who went missing?" Jacob asks. "You could have mistaken him for a douen. Did the person look scared?"

"The thing had no face. How am I supposed to know?"

But that's not true. Though the douen had no expression, I somehow knew it wasn't scared, but I don't know how to explain that to Jacob . . . or myself. "I saw something else. Something worse."

"What could possibly be worse than a douen in the forest?"

"A douen in the house. This morning, Peace's feet turned backward." I expect him to get faint or reach for his inhaler, but he gives me a very skeptical look instead.

"You mean, he turned his feet, like to a wall?"

"As in twisted backward. Like they were made out of Play-Doh."

"You're seeing douens everywhere now. Maybe you were—"

"No, I was not dreaming," I interrupt. "It's time we admit there's something supernatural going on. The Captain said this island is sick. Something about this place changes people. And Dr. Whisper has to be behind it."

Jacob shakes his head in denial. "That doesn't make sense, Serenity. You can't make douens in a lab. Douens are the souls of children who died before they're—wait, is Peace baptized?"

I pause and bite my lip. I distinctly remember going to the

church with my parents and watching the priest draw the watery cross on Peace's forehead.

My silence answers the question, and Jacob looks smug, but I give him a fixed stare. "I know what I saw. It seems impossible, but unbelievable things happen in that clinic."

"Timoteeth," we say together.

"You sure you didn't see anything at all when you were inside?"

"I told you: I was in the waiting area. Dr. Whisper took the rabbit, disappeared into some room, and came back a few minutes later. But you can't turn people into douens—that's not possible."

"We don't know what's possible until we get more info. Did you bring that folklore book with you?"

Jacob shakes his head.

"Think. You may remember something. What weaknesses do douens have? Are they allergic to anything? Does anything scare them?"

He seems clueless. "I—I don't know. I once read a story where they were scared of Papa Bois—the guardian of the forest. They pretend to be your parents and use their voices to lure you into the bushes."

I gasp as I remember my mother's melodious cries yesterday. The douen in the forest had plans for me from the very beginning.

"Maybe it's some forest magic that turns people into douens. Omigod, maybe John is a douen now too . . ."

He covers his face and I put my arm around him. "Don't think like that. Peace never went into the bushes, so that can't be it. There's still hope for John. Peace only changed after he started with treatments from Dr. Whisper. When we break into the clinic, we can look for evidence."

Jacob wipes his eyes angrily. "Evidence of what? Douens in test tubes?"

"I don't know! But if we find out how Dr. Whisper is turning Peace into a douen, it could help us figure out how to change him back. Or the coast guard could force Dr. Whisper to reverse the treatments."

"And what if the coast guard contacts Dr. Whisper directly? He would just lie. Even if we find something, no one would believe us."

I slump against a brick wall. "You're right. If only we could take photos or record proof. I left my camera in the forest."

We're running out of options, but I can't just sit around and play with papier-mâché zombies while Peace is turned into a monster. And I'm getting shipped off the island *tomorrow*. The clock is ticking.

"Maybe we can find where Dr. Whisper's keeping our phones," Jacob says, scratching his chin. "Newton said they were in some kind of safe, and he has a bunch of keys."

"Yes!" He winces as I slap his arm. "This is what we need. Solutions. When can we do this?"

"I still have to find his key card, but Dr. Whisper and Dad are doing rabbit inventory this morning. Maybe then?"

"Someone's gonna notice if I'm not washing a pile of gray uniforms by the standpipe."

My parents also banned me from filmmaking for the entire summer—which would have been devastating news if I didn't find out my brother was a douen a few hours ago.

"Hmm, if only you knew where to get recently washed gray tunics." He gives me a cheeky grin and my face brightens. Finally, it feels like we have some kind of plan.

We check the courtyard before we crawl from the hut. It's empty, but as soon as we turn the corner, we run smack-dab into Peace, James, and the Glitches, posed like a poster for a kiddie golf tournament.

We try to move around them, but they form a circle around us, everyone except Peace with gaping smiles on their faces. I feel like a rabbit surrounded by a pack of quiet dogs.

"Come play with me," the Glitches sing.

"Um, we have chores to do," I say, trying to hide the fear in my voice.

This time I try to shove past them, but it's like pushing against small garden statues. Jacob steels his shoulders and says in an authoritative voice, "Look, we don't have time for games." I expect the Glitches to giggle and run away like they normally do, but their expressions don't change.

"Just one game," Peace demands, putting his golf club on the ground. The Glitches follow suit in a sweeping, synchronized move. James drops his club and looks to his right. His face falls at the empty space beside him. He misses John.

Jacob glances at me and shrugs. They may not leave us alone until we agree.

"Okay, one round of mini golf, and that's it."

Peace gives a small grin that almost, almost reminds me of my real little brother. "We have another game in mind."

Before I know it, I'm pressed against a fake coconut tree, chosen as the designated "stoplight" in a game of Red Light, Green Light. Peace, Jacob, James, and the Glitches are in a horizontal starting line, about twenty yards away.

"Ready?" I ask, and everyone nods. I turn away from them.

"Red light, green light, one, two, three!"

I whirl around. Jacob has made the most strides, closer to me by about five yards. He nods at me; we want to win this game quickly. Peace, James, and the Glitches are close behind. Of course, I didn't hear or see anyone.

I turn my back to them again. "Red light, green light," and then I hear a slight noise on a tile. "One, two, three!" I finish quickly, and spin around, just in time to catch Jacob in mid-sprint. The others have barely moved and are frozen in position.

"You're out, Jacob," Peace says with a laugh. Jacob trudges away and sits by the picnic table to watch.

"One down, six more to go. I'm so gonna win," I tease them, hoping to unsettle them into making a mistake. It works. Everyone loses their creepy smiles and looks determined.

"Red light . . ." I say, drawing out the words, and then "green light, one, two, three!" in less than a second. I wheel around, guessing they'd only be a few feet away since they had more time to run.

I expected to catch at least one of them in the act.

I didn't expect to find all of them moving slowly toward me . . . without their faces.

TAKE 23—BREATHE

I know you're expecting filming instructions here, but it's still too surreal that kids with faces as blank as newly cut paper actors are advancing toward me.

So, director, if you can't capture the sound of blood rushing from my head to my toes, then make sure the actress's face expresses a fear so vast they wish their heart would stop beating.

Jacob's horror is much easier to show though, because he clutches at his chest, falls onto the ground, and starts to shake.

Everything inside me is screaming to run away, but I can't leave Jacob behind. I rush over and try to lift him, but he's a dead weight, struggling to breathe and making wheezing noises similar to air being let out of a balloon.

I fumble around in his pocket for the inhaler with one hand and try to drag him away with the other. We're sitting ducks for Peace and his douen gang, but instead of seizing the opportunity to pounce, they're like cats, taking their time to get to us and drawing out the angst as long as possible.

I find the inhaler, shove it into Jacob's mouth, and press down on the cartridge. It's loose. I press it again; nothing comes out.

Jacob coughs and claws at the inhaler.

"It's empty, Jacob, just breathe," I beg. His eyes widen in panic and he clutches his throat.

I move away but Jacob grabs my hand. "I need to get help," I tell him. There's a chance Peace and the gang will leave him alive, but Jacob's asthma can kill him for sure. Jacob points at something in the air, and when I follow his finger, I see the answer. Of course!

I close my eyes and take a deep breath.

When I scream, the sound meters turn red immediately. I keep going, though my throat starts to burn, hoping that the Glitches will short-circuit again, and that my parents or Uncle Newton or even Dr. Whisper will come running.

When I open my eyes, only one person is spasming on the ground.

James.

Jacob makes a strangled noise and tries to crawl to his brother, but his breathing gets even more choppy.

Peace's full face has returned and is twisted in a smug, ugly grin. But the faceless Glitches continue toward Jacob and me without a backward glance at James. Though the Glitches are a blank slate, there's movement under their skin; something is writhing in their flesh. Then lips appear on their empty faces, cracked at first but then smoothing into pink flesh. They smile and something wriggles out of their mouths.

Little bits of earthworm.

Now there are notes so high-pitched they can break glass. I would have shattered everything in a china shop if it was nearby. The scream slices through my throat like a knife. The Glitches still don't short-circuit, but they do stop advancing. They suck the worms into their mouths, and the rest of their faces fall into place like molded clay.

In the distance, Dr. Whisper bolts from the clinic, and my parents stumble out of the house. By the time they reach us, you'd never be able to tell that the children had lost their faces mere seconds before. Dr. Whisper clicks a black remote in his hand, and the alarms stop flashing.

Mum wraps me in her arms while Dr. Whisper pumps another inhaler into Jacob's mouth and Dad presses down on his chest. Jacob's eyes flutter open, and he grabs on to the inhaler while looking up at the Glitches in fear.

"Douen," he says in a weak voice. Dad and Dr. Whisper freeze. The Glitches huddle close to one another and pretend to be scared. Then in one coordinated motion, they point to James, whose unconscious body went unnoticed in the chaos. Dr. Whisper hurries over to him, checks his pulse, and then exhales.

"What happened here?" Dr. Whisper asks in a mat-ter-of-fact voice.

Before I can reply, Peace confesses.

"We were playing a game and Serenity saw a douen," Peace says, wiping away a tear. "Jacob got scared and couldn't breathe, and James fainted."

Dad lets out his long sigh and looks up to the gray clouds.

Mum, who was so sympathetic moments ago, snaps around in anger. "Serenity, this has got to stop! You could have killed someone with your creepy stories."

I want to say, *Peace and his friends took off their faces*, but who would believe me? Tears well up in my eyes, this time tears of anger, but I don't let them fall. I won't let them get the satisfaction. Maybe Uncle Newton will believe Jacob—actually, where is Uncle Newton?

Dr. Whisper notices his absence as well. "Can somebody find Newton and tell him to meet me in the clinic? We may need to fetch medical supplies."

"I'll get him," the Glitches say in unison, and hurry away with tiny steps, like dancers take in a ballet recital. After a few feet they turn around and giggle, but since everyone is focused on me, they don't notice at all.

Dr. Whisper gathers James in his arms in a surprisingly gentle manner, and Dad does the same with Jacob. His eyes become frantic when he realizes we're headed to the clinic.

There must be some kind of curse on that place; every time we plan to break in, somebody gets hurt.

"Don't talk," Dad says to Jacob, who is trying to form words. Though I can't understand, I know exactly what he wants to say—*Don't let Dr. Whisper treat me.* But there's nothing I can do except pray Jacob comes out the same way he went in. Hopefully Dr. Whisper won't liquefy his bones or inject him with some kind of douen serum. Jacob reaches out and grips my hand, so I'm forced to walk with everyone across the courtyard in uncomfortable, judgmental silence.

"There's nothing else we can do with you," Mum says, breaking the silence. "No other way we can punish you. Nothing else we can confiscate. Serenity, I don't know how else to help you."

I know I'm in serious trouble when Dad, Mr. Fix-It, has nothing to say.

"Maybe Dr. Whisper can help," Peace says in a small voice. "She's not a bad girl; Serenity just needs . . . treatment."

Dad's shoulders slump. "We talked about this, Peace. Dr. Whisper already has been more than hospitable, and we can't afford—"

"Maybe I can make another exception," Dr. Whisper interrupts. I gasp and look up at him.

"I could help her change . . . her ways." He examines me

like I'm a blue piece in a thousand-piece ocean puzzle. Is he imagining me without a face?

"Dr. Whisper," Mum says in a breathy voice, "we would be so grateful for your expertise."

"No," I reply in a loud, firm voice. I'm not letting him near me, especially after what he's done to Peace.

"Serenity!" Dad exclaims.

"You don't even realize what a great opportunity this is," Mum says.

"We can start tomorrow," Dr. Whisper says, not an ounce of emotion in his voice.

"I won't do it! And I'm leaving tomorrow!" I protest.

The facility doors slide open and I catch another glimpse of the Your Perfect Child poster. There's also a giant portrait of the Glitches on the wall in a far corner, with the slogan PERFECTION 100% GUARANTEED.

"I-I-I'm not allowed in the clinic." I wrestle my hand out of Jacob's and shoot him an apology with my eyes. I turn but there's nowhere to go. I'm like a bug in a jar with a few holes in the lid. In desperation, I sprint around the side of the building, ignoring my parents' soft cries behind me.

I run right up to the fence near the cliff, the absolute edge of the facility. Though I can't hear the ocean, the line of smoky blue in the distance helps me to breathe.

Inhale. Exhale.

How do douens breathe without noses? Do they not have

to breathe if, technically, they're dead? If I don't find a way to avoid Dr. Whisper's treatments, I may soon find out.

I press my face against the fence and close my eyes.

That's when I hear it . . . the dainty twinkle. My eyes fly open to see a silver butterfly, fluttering up the side of the cliff. It rests on a pointy barb at the top of the fence and flutters its wings, showing off the blue-and-purple crescent-shaped circles underneath. It's the same butterfly. Is it stalking me?

I follow it along the fence and pause at the edge of the fake grass. This time, there's no melodic voice trying to tempt me into the trees, but I still don't want to get any closer.

The butterfly seems to sense my apprehension. Just like in my dream, it flies down to the ground in front of the fence and lands on something black and shiny.

I squint and lean over and make out a white-checkered pattern.

My camera strap! Could it be? The silver butterfly waves its wings, then disappears into the trees. I take a deep breath and run toward the fence. It *is* my camera! Resting against a small branch just outside the fence.

With caution, I sneak up to the fence, surveying the area for any movement. It's all clear. No sounds. I close my eyes and listen. No music.

I jab four fingers through one of the small squares in the fence and grab the strap. The camera rakes against the wire as I yank it through the hole, leaving white dashes on its black exterior. I sprint back toward the clinic, clutching the camera close to my chest. Now I can show the recent footage to my parents, and prove to them that douens exist and I've been right all along.

I turn on my camera with trembling fingers but stop dead in my tracks when the screen lights up; it was at full charge yesterday, and today there's less than 25 percent. The camera shuts down automatically after five minutes, so there's no way it could have used all that juice.

I switch to the camera roll to view the recent recordings, but all of it is gone. Someone—or something—has deleted the footage.

TAKE 24—THE CLINIC

This is when I'd check to see how much time is left in this movie, because things have to get better now, right?

So many questions race through my head, but I push them aside. It doesn't matter how the camera got by the fence. All that matters is I have the means to expose Dr. Whisper's fraudulent program and save Peace. When I record evidence for the authorities, Dr. Whisper will soon be the one behind bars.

I just need to find a way into the clinic.

I shove the camera into the waist of my jeans and head to the house to hide it, but another thought stops me in my tracks.

Suppose the Glitches lied about getting Uncle Newton? Though he seems like the kind of parent who would let their children play with matches, I want to make sure Jacob's not alone with Dr. Whisper.

As usual, the courtyard is completely empty. For such a

small facility, people have a lot of places to disappear to, and I have no idea which house belongs to Uncle Newton.

I glance at them all, looking for one with any signs of equipment or cages in the window, but except for the chattel house with the blacked-out windows, they're all identical. The last thing I want to do is knock at a door and encounter something dangerous. I could be in a twisted game show, with the Glitches waiting behind door number five.

I decide to check the warren first. Sure enough, as soon as I get near the entrance, Uncle Newton comes outside carrying a tower of laundry so high it blocks his face.

"Uncle Newton!"

"Bethany, is that you? Can you give me a hand?" he replies with a muffled voice. But I don't move. I need to make sure his face is there.

"Uncle Newton, Jacob's in trouble," I say slowly, taking a few steps back, preparing to run. "He had an asthma attack."

"What!" Uncle Newton peers around the pile, sending a few tunics toppling to the ground. I exhale in relief when I see his alarmed face.

He drops the laundry into my arms as he hurries to the clinic. I follow him, relieved that he's taking the situation seriously for once.

"Which house is yours, Uncle Newton?" I call after him.

"Just rest them here in the lobby," he says impatiently, and waves his key card over the panel.

I've been invited right into the place I've been planning to break into. This time I don't hesitate.

I get goose bumps as soon as I step inside, and my breath becomes trapped in my chest. I'm overwhelmed by the strong smell of disinfectant. My eyes glaze over the Your Perfect Child posters on the wall and land on the uncomfortable-looking gray couch in the corner of the room.

I'm back.

Without another word, Uncle Newton disappears down a long white hallway.

I glance up at the roof, fully expecting to see the silver butterfly somewhere in the air, waving hello with its wings. It's not there. I purse my lips and decide to first search the reception desk on the other side of the room for my cell phone.

Luck is on my side; the drawers are still unlocked. I find a huge stack of yellowed calendars. Year 1854. The old receptionist must have been a hoarder. Unfortunately there's no sign of my phone, but I find an old crank radio/flashlight and an antique brass cross underneath the stack. *Music!* I snatch up the radio, bring it close to my chest, and then clip it onto my pocket.

I survey the long hallway. It's nothing like my dream. The walls are lit and instead of an eerie tunnel, it seems like a regular doctor's office. I'm both relieved and disappointed.

This is it: the moment of truth. I take a deep breath and press record on the camera.

My heart begs me to leave, but I instruct my feet not to listen. I quietly hum "The Ants Go Marching" as I walk down the hallway, capturing the shiny white walls and gray roof. I turn the corner and face the back doors of the clinic, with two brown doors on each side. This can't be right. This building should have several floors. Also, there's no sign of another panel or a NO ENTRY sign on either of the brown doors.

I check behind me one more time and then push down the handle on the door to the left. It gives the tiniest of clicks, like a clock hand.

Then there's blinding silver. Two rows of silver tables sparkle in the middle of the room, and glass drawers line the left and right walls. On the table are rows of glass cages with hairless rabbits curled up, surrounded by test tubes and glass jars filled with clear liquids.

I didn't know what to expect, but it was certainly not some kind of VIP rabbit laboratory. I pan the camera around, still recording while searching for a telephone or computer, but there's no sign of any communication devices. No safe in the wall either. All the drawers are filled with empty glass cylinders, beakers, and test tubes. This must be an equipment room.

I move closer to one of the glass cages, where a bald rabbit is lying down on its back, and notice a bump on its belly. It's a Mrs. Baldy! And about to have baby baldy rabbits. But the bulge has a strange circle arc, and as I lean in, the rabbit stretches, exposing more contours on its belly.

That's not a baby bump. It's a human ear! There's even a tiny black dot on the lobe for a piercing. Then the ear wiggles up and down like it's scratching an itch.

I yelp, backing away from the glass. My insides twist and churn, but I can't stop looking at it. All the other rabbits, now alert in the cages, press themselves up against the glass like they're begging me to save them. My frantic gaze takes in other rabbits with ears on their stomachs, one with a pinkie sticking out from its little paw, but the last rabbit, one with thick lips on the tips of its pointed ears, sends me bolting from the room.

I shove the door closed, and luckily it barely makes a sound. I pant against it, trying to control the urge to bolt from the clinic. My job's not done. The footage of mutant rabbits isn't enough to expose the truth. I still haven't found any clues about Peace's douen conversion or a way to contact the coast guard.

I stare at the other door in front of me, take another deep breath, and reach for the handle. It leads down into a staircase—not like the one in the house with the blacked-out windows—the area is well-lit, but the walls seem to be carved out of the rock with a chisel.

It's the tunnel from my nightmare . . . I grip the camera tighter, trying to will my trembling fingers to stay still.

Now that I'm here in real life, the tunnel is similar to the catacombs, the burial tombs in Paris, but without the skulls and bones in the walls. I just hope there's nothing dead down here.

I force myself to step inside, still filming everything, and whisper-whistle "The Ants Go Marching" to calm my nerves. The tunnel seems endless, and soon my lips become dry and my whistles become soundless breaths. I'm about to turn another corner when I hear voices up ahead. Good thing I'm dehydrated, else they would have heard me coming. Note to self: Spies shouldn't whistle.

"He's in stable condition now, but I've radioed the Captain to bring emergency medical supplies with him tomorrow. He should be here at sunrise."

Dr. Whisper! The other voice is too quiet for me to recognize, but I'm also distracted by the rush of relief through my veins. There's an opportunity to escape the island!

"Just keep the children away from the trees, especially the fruit ones. We can't afford for the douens to return to their natural form," Dr. Whisper responds.

Fruit? I was prepared for the douen cure to be laser treatment or some kind of magic ritual, but fruit? The solution to fixing Peace almost seems too simple. Who would have guessed an apple could thwart Dr. Whisper's nefarious treatments?

No wonder it's not allowed at the facility. If only I can get my hands on—wait—Jacob's secret fruit stash in the house with the blacked-out windows!

I do a fist pump and squeal in celebration. Out. Loud. I want to smack my head into the wall.

"Shh, did you hear that?" Dr. Whisper says, and I don't wait around any longer. There's nowhere to hide in this tunnel. I dash away as quickly and as quietly as I can.

TAKE 25—SOUL FOOD

Thankfully the back doors to the clinic slide open automatically, else I might have run face-first into them.

I head straight to the chattel house with the blacked-out windows, or as I now call it, the prison house.

I didn't find the radio to contact the authorities, and apart from the mutant bunnies, I haven't got any evidence of malpractice that could be used against the doctor. But my venture into the clinic wasn't a complete bust, because I've found out how to help Peace.

I need to secure that fruit.

I take a deep breath before entering the prison house, leaving the door slightly ajar to let in some light. Dr. Whisper has traumatized me for life. Now both Peace and I are afraid of the dark.

The clay pot is in the corner, just as Jacob described. I lift the lid and the sweet, fermented smell of fruit invades my nostrils. Unfortunately, there are only plum cores, seeds, and empty wrappers inside. I groan in disappointment, then cover the lid and rush to my house before I'm caught.

Questions zoom through my brain as I frantically search the kitchen for some kind of canned fruit, even chopped tomatoes. Who was Dr. Whisper talking to? Why would a rabbit need mouths on its ears? Suppose there's another mouth on Peace's belly too? I gag at the thought.

After raiding the cupboards, I lean against the counter and run my hands through my hair. There's no fruit in this house. I glance at the coconut trees in the distance and dread fills my chest.

I should have known it wouldn't be this easy.

There's only one place to find fresh fruit, but going into the heart of douen territory is too risky. Somehow I have to prevent Dr. Whisper from treating me—I just need to avoid him for one more day. It makes more sense to sneak on board the airship tomorrow, meet the Captain and tell him about the douens, and beg him to radio the police. He may even have some fruit on the boat.

But will the Captain believe the truth without any proof?

Dr. Whisper could easily make up some scientific reason for growing human ears on a bunny—searching for a cancer cure? Hearing loss? Either way, it still doesn't prove anything about his douen experiment with Peace.

I need more evidence.

I search through Peace's belongings for clues. Nothing but clothes, but there's a sharp, earthy smell coming from under the bed. I lift the bed skirt with reservation and peep underneath, praying that I don't stumble on Peace's face hanging from the bed coils.

The smell of pine invades my nostrils, and I pull out a brown bottle with clear liquid. Turpentine. Peace has moved on to oil painting. Some artists use the chemical to remove or mix oil paints. Sure enough, there's a whole new paint set and canvas stacked under the bed. When did he get more supplies? I wonder what else I missed.

The thought gives me an idea. I climb up on the dresser and position the camera on a ledge, toward our beds, activate the motion sensor, and put the trigger in my pocket. Now any movement will activate the camera. If Peace loses his face or his feet turn backward in this room, it will be captured on film.

As soon as I jump down from the dresser, the door opens. I stumble away from Peace's side of the room. Thankfully it's only Mum.

"I wanted to let you know Jacob is okay," she says, giving me a suspicious look. "Dr. Whisper is just keeping him under observation for a few hours."

"What about James?"

"James?" Mum avoids my eyes and my heart starts to beat a bit faster; Jacob can't handle losing another family member. "Jacob's brother?"

"Don't worry," she says, and starts to fix my rumpled bedsheet. "I'm sure he's fine. Good news though, the girls are still putting on the puppet show tonight. Then we're setting up for the party tomorrow."

"Party?"

"Your brother's birthday party, Serenity."

I freeze. In my efforts to stop Dr. Whisper, I had forgotten all about Peace's birthday. How is it possible for life to change so much in a few days?

"Let's go," Mum says, finally satisfied with the bed. "Time for evening meditation."

I can't fully suppress my groan.

Mum turns to me with a frown. "Serenity, we need to talk. You could have really hurt someone today. Dr. Whisper can help—"

"No way!" The mere idea makes my stomach twist in horror. How much longer will I be able to put them off? I shudder at the thought of being forced into the clinic, of having Dr. Whisper peer down at me while I'm strapped to a chair.

Mum decides I should stay in my room as punishment instead of going to meditation. I pretend to be devastated I can't join them. I need to stay out of Dr. Whisper's sight as much as possible.

Dad's still in a bad mood when everyone returns an hour later.

"You could have fixed dinner," he says in a cold voice. He hasn't forgiven me yet.

"I can do it," Peace says.

Dad rubs the top of his head, and Peace shoots me a gloating look. "Sure you can handle it, kiddo?"

"You don't have to be a genius to open a can, you know," I snap.

I have to collect water after being forced to apologize to Peace. By the time I return, everyone is seated and a plastic bowl of soup is waiting for me on the table. I'm surprised Peace set a place for me.

I shoot him one last scowl and as I lift the spoon to my mouth, I notice a quick change in Peace's face, so fleeting he himself doesn't seem to realize. I pause, but then when I bring the spoon to my mouth again, his face twitches. He sneezes and scratches his nose.

We all sit up in our seats. I've never heard him sneeze. Ever.

"Everything okay, sweetie?" Mum asks with furrowed eyebrows. She places the back of her hand on his forehead to check his temperature. Peace nods and continues to spoon the soup into his mouth.

But alarm bells ring again in my ears, and this time I listen. I swirl the spoon around the contents of the bowl: slimy noodles, pieces of unidentifiable greens, but as I lower my nose, I catch the unmistakable scent of sweet pine that I can't quite place. My eyes dart up just in time to catch Peace watching me, and he quickly looks away.

The turpentine! That's where it's from. I remember the red-and-yellow warning label and the DO NOT INGEST sign on the back of the bottle.

My fingers tighten on the spoon. Could it be? Is Peace trying to poison me? It's hard to digest that my sweet brother, who once guided a cockroach out of the house rather than smash it with a shoe, would now be capable of murder. Does this mean Peace is becoming more douen than human? I push away the bowl with trembling hands.

"You're not hungry?" Dad asks, and reaches for my bowl.

"Stop!" I yell without thinking, and knock it out of his hands. The bowl bounces on the table, soup and noodles flying all over Dad, and worse, his tablet. Dad yelps—an actual yelp, about fifty-five decibels—and leaps up with the tablet.

I grab a dish towel, trying to wipe some gunk from his face. I don't want him to accidentally ingest anything. I glance at Peace, and he actually looks scared. There's an uncontrollable twitch on his cheek, and he clutches his face in disbelief.

"I'm sorry, Ren," Peace says, and then slaps a hand over his mouth.

"You have nothing to apologize for, son. Serenity, what is wrong with you?" Dad asks, yanking the towel out of my hands and wiping the screen.

What can I say? That Peace is not Peace, and whatever he is poisoned my soup and is out to kill me? "I—I wasn't done," I stutter.

Mum gently takes my hand, leads me to the bedroom, and sits me on the bed.

"I can't do this anymore," Mum whispers sadly. "It's too much." She grabs a suitcase and starts to throw clothes into it.

"Are we all leaving?" I ask, hope rising inside me.

"Peace is," Mum says, zipping the bag shut. "You're going to stay here alone tonight and really think about everything you've done."

I want to pull out my hair. If only she knew how much thinking I've had to do since I arrived at this facility. "Please, Mum, you don't understand," I say in a pleading voice.

She stops at the door and glances back at me, her eyes filled with hurt and confusion. She drops her shoulders and places my iPod on the dresser.

"Your father and I have made a decision. Tomorrow, you start your sessions with Dr. Whisper."

"Mum, please, you can't—"

But she closes the door before I can finish. Then the lock clicks—the sound of the final nail in my coffin.

Dr. Whisper will wipe my brain tomorrow. Who knows what memories he'd leave with me? Or he could turn me into a douen! Would I have a total personality change, like Peace?

Suddenly I understand. Dr. Whisper never intended for me to simply leave Duppy Island tomorrow, not with all I've witnessed. Dread bubbles in my stomach.

Tomorrow, Serenity Noah, daughter, sister, filmmaker as you know her . . . may no longer exist.

TAKE 26—A CHANGE OF HEART

I pace up and down the room, yelling along to my spouge mash-ups, hoping that my anger will break the door.

I still can't believe Peace tried to poison me. And if he could do that to me, the person he loves most, then no one is safe. Not even Mum and Dad. Suppose they're out there eating turpentine-laced soup right now? I can't give up; I have to find a way out of this room and get fruit from the forest . . . tonight.

I yank at the door again, hoping that it somehow unlocked from when I last tried it thirty seconds ago.

I check under Peace's bed, and sure enough, the bottle of turpentine is missing, leaving only the lingering smell of pine in its place. I hit Peace's pillow in frustration, and a small paper foot pops out from underneath.

I carefully move the pillow and see a new paper family underneath it.

Mum and Dad are roughly cut, as if Peace was making the figures under duress, but he still managed to detail their matching dashiki design. There's a new paper Serenity wearing headphones as well, but that's not what gets my attention.

Peace has carefully cut out two Peaces. One of them has painted details: a red smile and a huge red heart in its chest. The other Peace has no features at all, and there are clumps of white paint on the paper; he deliberately painted it white.

I lie in bed, holding the two Peaces in the air, and a second later, the lights from the facility come on, shining through the two paper Peaces and making the red heart even more prominent. I stare at them for a long time, and then all the frustration, exhaustion, and confusion is too much. I close my eyes for a second.

Clink.

My eyes fly open. I'm curled up under a blanket; I must have fallen asleep.

Clink.

I leap from my bed as a white shape hits the steel bars on the window and becomes stuck in one of the squares. It's a papier-mâché zombie!

I press my face against the steel to see Jacob outside, his face grayer than the tunic.

"Jacob! Thank God you're okay. Dr. Whisper didn't do anything to you, right?"

He puts a finger to his lips and gestures for me to lower my voice. "I'm not allowed to talk to you anymore."

"But I'm not the one who nearly killed you!"

"Shhh!" Jacob says again, and though I know he's right, the sound still irritates me. "Everyone is in the common room, but we still have to be quiet."

"I have news," we both say at the same time.

"You first," I tell him.

"I overheard Dr. Whisper talking in the clinic, about douens." He shivers and pauses.

"It's okay, go on."

Jacob takes a breath. "Dr. Whisper is lying. He knows there are douens in the forest, but they can't get into the compound. The lights scare them away."

"But the kids here turned into douens in broad daylight."

"I know, but maybe they're special. Clearly the baptism thing doesn't matter here. James is baptized too," he says.

He's right. The douen I saw in the forest seemed different from Peace and the Glitches. More natural. Like when you buy coconut water from vendors at the side of the road versus the bottled brands in the supermarket.

"He also said something about a final transformation at midnight," Jacob adds. "I don't understand what it means, and he left the room before I could learn more."

Final transformation at midnight? *On Peace's sixth birthday.*

Some of the dots finally start to connect, and there's a sick feeling of worry heavy in my gut.

"How old are the Glitches?" I ask in a choked whisper. Please, don't let me be right . . .

Jacob seems confused by the question. "Seven, I think—no, six! They celebrated their birthday a few weeks ago. Why do you ask?"

My chest constricts, and for a moment, I can barely breathe, let alone speak. Dr. Whisper's douen transition becomes permanent when the child turns six years old. *This is why he has to monitor kids until they reach that age. Which means I have*—I check my watch—*three* hours to find some fruit and save my brother.

I'm about to explain all this to Jacob, but then to my dismay, I realize it's too late to help his brothers. I can't tell him my suspicions, not just yet.

"No reason, I was just wondering," I reply, hating myself for lying.

I tell Jacob about the conversation I overheard, the fruit cure, and the cherries in the clearing in the forest. "We need to get the fruit *tonight*," I stress, and then hastily add, "while they're distracted by the puppet show."

"Okay."

I stare at him in surprise. I expected more resistance. "*You* are just 'okay' to go into the forest?"

"Of course not! You know I always follow the rules!" Tears well up in his eyes. "I ate all the fruit. All of it. We had the cure right in our hands."

"It's not your fault," I reassure him. "You didn't know."

Still, it's so unlike Jacob to want to run to danger. This could be a trap. Dr. Whisper could have messed with his DNA, and he's leading me to my doom. I'm not sure if I can trust him, but I don't have a choice.

"How did Jackie Opel die?" I ask suddenly.

"What does that have to do with anything?"

"Just answer."

"In a car crash."

He passed the test. I'm going to have to take a leap of faith. "I'm locked in. Get me out of here."

I grab my backpack and my eyes zero in on the two paper Peaces on the dresser. I try to solve the puzzle, but there are so many missing pieces.

The doorknob jiggles, and then the door opens to reveal a triumphant-looking Jacob with a pocketknife.

I push the thoughts aside again and focus on the matter at hand.

We need to find some fruit.

We try our best to stay out of sight, keeping close to the perimeter and crawling past the common room. The only signs of a show are quiet giggling and tall shadow puppets on the wall. Finally we take a chance and sprint across the courtyard to the back of the clinic.

I pause again by the fence, looking out at the trees, only visible because of the facility's lights. How far will the beams reach before it goes into total darkness? This is a suicide mission. It's going to be difficult to find the cherry-tree clearing at night, but I have to try. If it's a choice between my life or my brother's, I'll choose Peace's every single time.

"Let's do this?" Jacob says, in a tone that seems like he's open to us changing plans. I nod, and together, we climb over the fence and enter the forbidden forest.

TAKE 27—THE HAIRY TREES

At first, neither of us speaks, keeping our mouths tightly closed to hide the chattering of our teeth. Though the facility lights still brighten the path ahead, we grip our flashlights, pointing them in front of us like swords.

The smell of fresh dirt is even stronger at night, and the music of the forest is on full blast. The trees are alive; you can almost hear them breathing. When it starts to get a little darker, we turn on the beams.

I feel a tiny bit of relief when we get to the circle of coconut trees. We're on the right track so far. It's only been about ten minutes. If everything goes to plan, I will be shoving fruit in Peace's mouth within the hour. I shine the light on the ground, hoping to spot a fallen coconut. It lands on a row of freshly made mounds, curved with such precision they look like they're sculpted.

I stop Jacob from going closer. The last time I encountered a strange mound it came to life, so I'm not taking any chances.

I grab his hand and we slowly back away from the mounds, careful not to disturb them. Jacob points the light behind us to make sure it's safe, and I don't turn around until the mounds are out of sight.

We enter into the section with the tall trees with hairy vines. It's a different path from the one I took before, but I'm hoping we soon spot a fruit tree. I can smell the sweetness in the air.

The vines are piled on the forest floor, and it's like walking on carpet. And it's odd, but my eyes adjust really well to the darkness. The longer I spend in the forest, the easier it is to distinguish the shadows from one another. We find a new bumpy path between the trees.

"This is probably not a good time to talk about our horror movie, right?" Jacob whispers.

"No, it isn't," I reply, still surveying the area for coconuts, cherries, soursops, any fruit at all. "But we're already making bad decisions."

"Okay, good, because I finally figured out what we should name the zombie workout class. Zomba."

I snort. "That's ridiculous, but I like it."

"Yeah, the catchphrase could be 'shed that dead weight.' "

It takes a lot of effort to maintain my composure. It's probably not the best idea to laugh while walking through a haunted forest at night.

I get serious and check my watch again. Two and a half hours before midnight. "Maybe we can learn something from those characters who die first in movies," I say, trying to ease my anxiety.

"Go on," Jacob replies.

"So, rule number one. Always look down when running, because you *will* trip up on a vine."

"Good point," he says with a serious voice. "Let's not be cliché."

I run through all the horror movies in my brain, and it actually eases the tension. "Number two. If you need to escape quickly, climb a tree. No one ever expects that."

"What if you can't climb?"

"Then hope that you're best friends with the hero, because then they'll distract the monster to save you."

"That's what best friends are for, right?" he asks, ducking under a large vine blocking the path. I open my mouth to give a clever retort, but then I pause.

"I don't know. I've never actually had one," I answer truthfully.

He opens his mouth to reply, but then I bring a finger to my lips.

There's an airy melody up ahead. In reflex, I pull Jacob behind a thick curtain of vines and we hold our breath. There's something coming toward us for sure; I can make out a flash of silver against the foliage.

"It's John!" Jacob whispers, and he tries to leap out from the vines, but I stop him. "Wait," I whisper. He frowns but thankfully he doesn't move.

A ball of silver butterflies flutters above John, as bright as a full moon, shedding enough warm light to show his gray tunic hanging on to him in shreds, but he doesn't seem injured at all. Actually he's having the time of his life, spinning around on his bare heels and frolicking in the vines. The butterflies twist above him like a butterfly halo. We watch as he hugs every tree as he gets closer. John doesn't make a sound, not even a giggle.

Finally he's close enough for us to see his face, and as I suspected, nothing is there except his mouth. It opens wide in delight as he twirls a vine around his arm. I cover Jacob's mouth with my hand in case he can't hold in his scream, but he's frozen in shock, not even breathing.

I instinctively reach for my camera, then remember I left it on the ledge in the bedroom.

John doesn't notice us at all, but he offers a piece of vine to the empty space next to him. His mouth turns into a frown and he drops the vine on the ground, then continues on to the next tree, running his hands along the bark and giving it the tightest hug, before disappearing into the bushes.

Jacob and I both stare at the spot until it's clear that John isn't coming back. Jacob starts to heave as tears roll down his cheeks.

How can I tell him it may be too late for his brothers now? I could be wrong. Maybe the fruit will still change them back to normal.

I take his hand in mine and squeeze. "We'll find the cherries, okay? We'll help him."

Jacob nods and wipes his tears away. We step back out onto the path and then jerk to a stop.

In front of us is a gang of douens, at least twelve of them, in a semicircle-like battle position. My whole body starts to shake. I would scream, but I think I would swallow my tongue. These douens sound like the whisper of wind through the trees; there's no way I could have known they were coming. They're all different sizes, from skinny to plump, though none of them are as tall as we are. But unlike the douen I saw yesterday, their skin is a dull red ocher—the color of dried blood.

In a synchronized move, the douens lift their right hands and point their fingers at us.

"Run!" I shout.

We tear through the vines, trying not to slide on the wet leaves. Behind us, there's an echo of "Run!" in a chorus of voices, and in my panic it's difficult to focus on the path ahead. Our beams seem to illuminate the same patch of bush.

It feels like the forest is moving with us, with vines and branches suddenly blocking our way and the mud shifting like waves in the sea.

"This way!" Jacob says, grabbing my hand, and we crash through another wall of leaves and into another area full of towering hairy trees. A vine whips at our clasped hands. We both yelp and dash in opposite directions.

I duck behind one of the trees and twist my head around for Jacob, but he's nowhere in sight. The gang of douens pop into the clearing and survey the area, their fingers still pointed in front of them. I start to climb the tree and then have to bite down on my tongue to stop myself from screaming.

The trees are "hairy" with pointed black thorns.

I try to ease my hand off the thorns along the bark, but they come alive at the taste of my blood and curve into my flesh. Tears come to my eyes as the barbs shift and stand at attention inside my hand.

"Ow!"

That isn't me; the sound comes from the other side of the clearing.

Jacob.

My heart sinks when I realize he must have tried to climb a tree too. The douens echo the cry, and it sounds like a pack of dogs howling in the night.

I take the opportunity to yank my hand from the tree with the smallest of grunts. I slide to the ground and take a peek. The douens have converged around a terrified Jacob, closing in on him like sharks around fresh bait.

He throws a rock at the tallest douen, but it bounces off his chest like a rubber beach ball. He doesn't make a sound, but the rest of the douens leap at Jacob at the same time.

"Leave me alone!" Jacob yells. "Don't hurt me!"

Two douens lift him into the air, and he struggles but they have iron grips. A tear runs down my cheek, and I squeeze the mud between my fingers. The hero would distract the douens right now to save their best friend. I want to do something, but I'm so scared.

I am not the hero.

"Serenity!" he yells, just before some of the douens disappear with him into the trees.

The other douens echo my name and continue to search behind nearby trees. I close my eyes and cover my ears to block out the sound. There's nowhere to run; it's only a matter of time until I'm discovered.

Then a whistle penetrates the whispers of my name. A cowboy whistle.

My eyes fly open and I see a brown douen in the bushes a few feet away. Even though he has no eyes, I can feel him peering into my soul.

It's the first douen from the forest.

I prepare to run, but the douen holds up a muddy palm and puts a finger to his mouth. Maybe it's because I'm desperate for help as the gang of douens closes in, but my heart tells me I can trust him. He keeps his palm up for a few more seconds and then beckons for me to follow.

I hesitate for a moment before dashing across to the area, leaping into the bushes behind him.

TAKE 28—TRILL

I push through the bushes, nursing my injured hand. The douen is careful to leave a clear path for me, pointing out the sharp branches. He slides through the crevices, his coconut-leaf skirt blending into the foilage as we move farther and farther away from the whispering.

Eventually the chant of my name fades away, making space for the douen's gentle music. Imagine the echo of a guitar note before it disappears, a moment before the audience applauds. It is so familiar and captivating; I blame the sound for why I'm letting myself be guided by a faceless Pied Piper, ignoring the fact that it's getting darker and darker ahead.

I try to recall everything about our encounter yesterday. Once I push past the fear and shock of seeing something with no face, I realize the douen didn't do anything besides look scary. There was no growling, no bared teeth, no hostile behavior. It just stood there and whistled. And unless I hallucinated, it whistled to me again when I was locked up.

Suddenly there's nothing but air in front of me. I drop about two feet down and throw my hand in front of my body to break the fall. I crash onto the ground and clench my teeth, waiting for the pain. But it never comes.

I brush the mud from my hand and flex my fingers. There are no signs of the cuts; it's like the punctures were never there.

I get to my feet, still frowning at my hand, and squint in the darkness. I dropped the flashlight somewhere, but I know this place even though I can't see it.

The douen whistles, and the air comes alive. At least a hundred butterflies spread their wings in the trees, and their shimmer lights up the area like stars. My breath catches in my throat, and I tilt my face up to the trees, turning around in a circle and getting lost in the butterflies' dainty fairy music.

I don't have my camera, but it doesn't matter—no lens can capture this magic; be sure to hire the best visual-effects artist money can buy to accurately depict this scene.

I'm in the cherry-tree clearing. If the cherries hum during the day, at night their song is at the climax, the energy buzzing through the air. I'm so close to getting the cure for Peace; only one thing stands in my way.

The douen comes within an arm's reach, opens his mouth, and whispers my name. I cower, but then I notice the movements of his lips. They are out of sync with "Serenity." It reminds me of those English-dubbed kung fu movies.

If I were scoring this scene, there'd be a loud guitar strum as the camera zooms in on the douen's mouth. The longer I stare at his lips, the clearer the words form in my brain.

You are safe here.

"I'm safe here? So you're not gonna drink my blood?"

The douen stops speaking, and, I kid you not, clutches at his chest like a nosy neighbor who just heard the most delicious gossip.

He opens his mouth again and echoes the word *safe*, but I tune out the sound and focus on his lips. Now I can understand him, give or take a few words.

You get me. I knew it.

"What's your name?" I ask, stepping closer to see his lips more clearly.

Drill.

Drill? That can't be right. I repeat the question, but slower.

The douen taps on his chest again and this time, there is no echo when he moves his lips.

Trill.

"Trill?" I ask, and he nods, looking quite pleased to hear it out loud.

"Trill, can you help Jacob? Can you save him?"

The douen shakes his head and lowers his face to the ground so I can't read his lips. He echoes Jacob's name and some of the butterflies shift in the trees, flapping their wings in near unison. The movement looks like a line of falling silver dominoes. The air turns somber and the butterflies seem to pay a tribute.

The douen lifts his head, the echo of "Jacob" still in the air. *He is lost.*

He's gone . . . and it's my fault. All because I advised him to climb a tree. Suppose he's still calling out my name or hoping that I've gone to get help?

"Please," I plead. "What do the red douens want? We can make a deal. Can I use the cherries to save him?" But no matter the question, the douen gives the same answer.

He is lost. He is lost. He is lost.

"So what's stopping the red douens from finding me, then?" I yell in frustration, and immediately regret it when the douen flinches and several butterflies fly away, taking their light with them.

The douen says a stream of words, and it takes a long time to decipher them.

You are safe. Stay here. Sacred place. Butterflies are life. Butterflies are death.

The butterflies are both life and death? That makes absolutely no sense, and my rising frustration makes it harder to understand him through the echo of Jacob's name.

"Can you just be quiet?! Please!" I cover my ears, and the douen closes his mouth. He actually looks offended; I recognize that stance—the tense shoulders, head cocked to the side and mouth pushed up to the area where the nose should be.

In this bizarro forest, I've swapped places with my parents, and the douen is me.

I sigh in shame—a very Dad-like sigh. This is too much. I need to think. I reach into my backpack and pull out my iPod, eager for music to reclaim my identity. Serenity Noah. A filmmaker with no camera. Unable to record history. Trapped in a forest with a douen.

My body relaxes as soon as the spouge beats caress my eardrums, and I sit on the grass, unraveling my thoughts to Jackie Opel's remix of "Higher and Higher." The douen cocks his head to the side again and pokes the headphones with a finger. His mouth imitates the rhythm of the bass.

"You like music?" I ask, pulling out one of the headphones. "It will be loud," I warn, remembering how he reacted earlier when I shouted. He ignores me and pushes the headphone into his ear, little bits of mud falling from the side of his head.

If he had eyes, I'm sure they would have flown open to their fullest. The douen stumbles back, the movement yanking the other headphone from my ear, and his arms flap about at his sides like he's trying to take off in flight.

I rush to help him but he swats my hand away, his mouth falling open and quivering. Then his entire body goes rigid, as if he's been plunged in cold water. I try to remove the headphone again, but then his shoulders start to shake. And the douen starts to whistle the melody.

His trill matches the lyrics perfectly; he masters the rhythm after only hearing it for a few seconds. He shimmies around the clearing with my iPod and wheels around in circles.

As he dances past a cherry tree, I remember my mission and check my watch. Where did the time go? I have *an hour* to pick some of the fruit and get back to Peace. I head over to the trees while the douen is distracted, grab a few of the lowest-hanging cherries, and push them in my backpack.

But then I notice a section of the clearing with scattered rocks and several mounds of dirt. Behind the mounds is a tall curtain of pale vines, swaying even though there's no wind.

Curious, I creep over to the area. Some of the mounds have plants shooting up from them. A green caterpillar sits on one of the larger plants, feasting on the leaves. In fact, most of the plants are infested with caterpillars; a few of them hang from the branches in cocoons.

A silver light flutters inside one of them, and I gasp as a silver butterfly bursts from its sack, the pink, yellow, and gold color patterns under its wings glittering brighter than jewels. The new butterfly flutters through the curtain of vines.

I follow it behind the curtain and would have dropped into a sinkhole if not for the butterfly's light. The butterfly lands on a piece of rotting wood jutting from the ground, bringing enough glow for me to realize it's a cross . . . with the name "Elijah" scratched into it.

This is no sinkhole. It's a grave for the kid who went missing.

Chills run down my spine and my insides do a somersault as I notice dozens of shadowed crosses in the murkiness.

This is a trap.

A heavy hand lands on my shoulder and yanks me back through the vines. The douen frowns at me and removes the headphones from his ears.

"Please, what do you want?" I ask, trying to pry his hands away, but his nails dig deeper in my shoulders. He brings his face closer to mine, so close I notice there's no breath coming from his mouth. He smells of dust and soil.

The lights. The light. Kill the lights.

He is dead. A talking dead thing. The realization hits me like a ton of bricks. How could I have let down my guard so easily?

"I—I—I don't know how," I stutter. It's strange how someone so small and frail-looking could be so strong. I bet he could shove me underground with one push. Maybe that's what happened to Elijah . . .

Trill stamps his foot, shifting some of the dirt from a nearby mound. *Kill the lights.*

"Please don't hurt me!" I cry. Jacob's information was right. The lights are the only things keeping the forest douens away from the facility.

I ease my hand behind me and grab the windup radio

from the side of the backpack. I hope it still works. I press the power button, a bright LED light flickers on, and I shine it in Trill's face.

He recoils and flings his arms in front of his face, and I use the moment to escape back into the forest.

TAKE 29—THEY'RE ALL GONE

If I survive this experience, I could make some extra cash giving guided tours of this haunted forest, because my instincts seem to know the way back to the compound.

After I realize Trill isn't chasing after me, I start to listen for the red douens' wind. My gut tells me to follow the silence. I keep expecting Trill to step out of the trees, but I never feel his presence. I keep the flashlight in hand to scare off the creatures, now that I know artificial light is a weakness—at least for the douens in the forest.

I find my way back to the coconut-tree clearing and beam the light around, hoping to see a disheveled Jacob with a grand tale about his daring escape, but the beam only reveals footprints in the mud . . . and some of them are backward!

I can't abandon Jacob again. After I help Peace, I have to try to save him too.

With renewed determination, I push through the bushes until I'm in range of the facility lights, climb over the fence, and rush to the common room.

I burst inside but there's no one there. The half-decorated room has a haunted, eerie aura. The gray streamers droop down the walls underneath a gray HAPPY BIRTHDAY, PEACE hand-painted banner. There's a dusty three-layer plaster cake on a table, next to five dingy sock puppets with googly eyes stuck onto the heels. Looks like I would have missed a terrible party.

I race to the warren next, and thankfully, Uncle Newton is there, sitting at his work space with his hammer.

"Serenity," he says sadly when he notices me. It's the first time he's gotten my name right.

"Gone." Uncle Newton moans and shakes his head. "They're all gone."

My heart sinks. Am I too late? There are still thirty minutes till midnight. "What do you mean?" I ask, a tremble in my voice.

He rests his head on top of the hammer and motions around the room. "At least they were happy."

I finally notice all the cages are empty. Where are the rabbits? But I don't have time to worry about that now. I need to find Peace, but I can't leave without warning Uncle Newton.

"The douens took Jacob."

He's still gazing at the empty cages with mournful eyes. "What do you mean?"

I step farther inside the hut. "We went into the forest, Uncle Newton. I know we shouldn't have, but we did. And the douens captured Jacob. You need flashlights, torches, matches, any lights to save him. My parents will help if you ask them, I know they will."

Then this vacant look comes over his face. "Who is Jacob?" he asks.

"Your son!" I yell, too frustrated to care about any sound meters.

Uncle Newton bows his head. "I don't have any sons. No one for you to play with."

I am speechless, but before I can respond, Uncle Newton snaps his head and points the hammer at me. "I know! I'll take you to the clinic. There are lots of children there."

I start to back away to the exit, but Uncle Newton latches on to my arm with extreme delight. "Felicity, you'll make loads of friends. It'll be fun."

I grab one of the empty cages with my free hand and yank it with all my strength. It comes tumbling from the wall, bringing a few others along with it. Uncle Newton releases his grip to shield his face from the falling cages, and they crash onto the floor.

Ninety decibels.

I run out of the hut, expecting to see the red lights blaring outside, but it's still silent. I take a deep breath and scream into the air. It echoes in the silence.

Someone has turned off the alarms. Once upon a time I would have been relieved, but now I've never felt more vulnerable.

I reach into the front of my backpack, pushing my hand into the pouch for the cherries. If there is another attack, I need to be armed and ready to shove the fruit into Peace's mouth.

But the pouch is empty.

"No, no, no, no, no," I moan. I bring the backpack to my chest, frantically plowing into the space. Then my hand goes right through the pouch; there's a giant hole along the seam.

"This can't be happening, this can't be happening," I repeat. I search the area, hoping to spot even one red cherry on the ground. My vision gets blurrier and blurrier as hopeless tears flood my eyes.

"Felicityyyyy," Uncle Newton calls.

I gasp and dash to my chattel house, shutting the door behind me. The cushioned lining mutes the slam. I go to lock the door but then remember there's no lock.

"Mum! Dad!" I yell, but their room is empty.

What do I do? I'm out of options.

This is the "all is lost moment" in the film, right? When the hero runs out of options and has to look deep within themselves to find a solution and get a clearer picture of—a picture!

I rush to the other bedroom and climb Peace's dresser for my camera. Thankfully it's still there, but there's not much charge left, less than 10 percent.

I check the last bit of footage. At first, there's nothing

except me in bed sleeping. Then a shadow appears in the corner of the frame.

I hold my breath, but it's only Mum, picking up socks off the floor and putting my sneakers aside. I've never thought about how everything magically returned to its place. She gives the shoes a whiff and gags; anyone who brings dirty shoes close to their face deserves what they get.

She covers me with the blanket, making sure I'm tucked in, and then lifts the two Peaces off the bed. She smooths out the paper brothers and places them on the dresser. Then she opens my sketch pad and starts to look at the zombie storyboards I'd been sketching. I want to scream "That's private!" and also "What do you think?" at the same time.

Mum's shoulders start to shake—with laughter! She gestures at the door and Dad appears, and she shares the sketchpad with him. I try to read their lips, but it's too blurry, so I focus on their body language instead. Dad takes his time to analyze, and swats Mum's hand away when she tries to turn the page before he's done.

A warm feeling floods my body as I watch. Then the camera battery turns red, warning me about the low power.

When I turn off the camera, my cheeks are wet. I never realized how important it was for my parents to like my stories. I move over to Peace's bed to get the paper Mum and Dad. I want to keep everyone in my pocket as a reminder of what I'm fighting for.

But the paper parents are gone.

I check under his bed but only see piles of canvas, including the white painting with the red slashes. I examine the brushstrokes again. Mum and Dad paid attention to my work and enjoyed it, even though horror isn't their thing. I owe Peace the same favor.

The brushstrokes are in perfect alignment, and you can tell he took his time placing the globs of paint on the canvas; it looks like a wicker-chair pattern. There's something beautiful in its simplicity, yet the longer I stare at it the more complex it becomes.

I hold the canvas in the air and turn it around. The light illuminates the imprint of the brushstrokes at the back of the painting to reveal words in the pattern:

Help me.

A message . . . from Peace?

My brother's still in there! Fighting Dr. Whisper's treatments. I think about how he lost control of his face when I was about to swallow turpentine. He was trying to warn me.

I have to find him and my parents. I don't have the fruit, but I won't let them go without a fight.

To my relief, as soon as I step out of the bedroom, Mum and Dad appear in the hallway, wearing party hats and their finest dashikis. They both seem startled to see me.

"What are you doing here?" Mum asks.

"Mum, something terrible has happened. Don't be mad,

but I went into the forest and douens kidnapped Jacob, and before you tell me there're no such things as douens, look at this." I wave the back of Peace's canvas in their faces.

"Be careful with that!" Dad exclaims. "That's our son's painting. It's an amalgamation of pi signs."

"I thought it represented infinity," Mum says, taking the painting and turning it upside down.

"Listen to me! You know Peace has been acting strange. Dr. Whisper is turning him into a douen. We have to stop him, right now. We don't have a lot of time."

"Are you lost?" Mum asks, ignoring my monologue. "What's your name?"

I gape at her, and when I turn to Dad, he gives me his polite smile reserved for ex-neighbors who try to initiate conversation.

They don't remember me.

Just like how Uncle Newton doesn't remember Jacob.

"It's me," I reply in a small voice. "Serenity. Your daughter."

"Poor thing is confused. Come here, sugar dumpling." Mum kneels and gathers me in her arms. I return her hug and tears flow down my cheeks.

"Doesn't she look familiar, Adisa?" she says.

Dad shakes his head with pity but focuses on his tablet. "Maybe you can take her to Uncle Newton or Dr. Whisper. They'll know how to help her."

Dad gives me two pats on my head before heading into the bedroom.

"Dear, dear, don't cry. We'll find your parents," Mum says, wiping away my tears with the silk material.

She doesn't recognize a face that is almost a reflection of her own. Dr. Whisper has them brainwashed; they're safer here away from him.

"Um, I don't need help. I just—" I pause, clearing the frog in my throat. "Dr. Whisper wanted me to warn you that there've been some, um, wild animals loose. Best to stay inside and lock all doors and windows till he takes care of it."

"Oh dear, will do. Dr. Whisper knows best."

You know when you watch a movie and guess all the plot twists? The audience would have figured out that Dr. Whisper's been messing with my parents' heads a long time before I did. I have to get answers, and all roads lead to one place: the metal door in the clinic.

Mum places her hands on my cheeks and gives them a little squeeze. Before entering the bedroom, she stops in the doorway and narrows her eyes.

"Serenity, are you a sprinter, by any chance?"

I force a smile. "No."

"Hmm, that's odd." She shrugs. "There's a voice in my head. It's telling you to run."

TAKE 30—DÉJÀ VU

This time I don't race across the courtyard.

I take my time, glaring at the fake coconut tree, the meditation space, the rabbit hut, the common room, the gray tiles, all with a cutting eye, as if daring them to stop me.

The fear is still inside, but it's nestled under a wave of anger, fatigue, and determination. If I'm gonna die, I'm gonna go down fighting.

I wave my hand over the keypad, expecting it to turn red and for a cage to drop over me, but I'm not ready for the doors to open with a soft puff. That lack of drama threw off my whole bravado.

Before I head into the tunnel, I decide to check the rabbit lab again, just in case. The glass cages now have triple the amount of rabbits, and I waste no time setting them free. The bunnies leap outside and race through the open door.

It's nice to see some things escape, even if I don't.

I'm about to leave when I notice one rabbit still in its cage. Timoteeth.

"Come on, run for it," I whisper. Despite my urging, Timoteeth refuses to budge. Reluctantly I leave him behind but keep the cage open in case he changes his mind.

In my nightmare, the tunnel seemed endless, but it's not long before I'm facing the metal door with the NO ENTRY sign. Though the fear inside threatens to consume me, I need to finally see the end of the nightmare. Once I open this door, I can never fear the unknown again.

I release a breath and then wave my hand over the panel, not expecting it to open. But it does. A red dot appears and there are two quiet beeps, the bird's chirps.

The door opens with a soft hiss.

I peep through the crack. It's another sparkling laboratory.

Rows of silver machines and glass shelves with test tubes, beakers, and other lab equipment line the tables. I push the door open an inch wider and spot the Glitches on the floor in birthday-cone hats with their disturbing smiles, staring up at a large screen—almost twice the size of Gran's fifty-inch TV. But there are no game shows on, only a large countdown with fifteen minutes remaining. I check my watch.

Fifteen minutes before midnight.

"Hello?" I whisper, but they seem frozen in time. As still as mannequins. I never thought I'd wish for their creepy, synchronized attention.

I turn on the camera and step into the room, trying to capture as much as I can before the battery dies. When I do a 360 pan, I see pulsating cocoons along the back wall. They look like gigantic green beehives with spots of silver. And, attached to a machine by a hundred tubes, are two unconscious Peaces.

I lower the camera as my knees buckle. I think I might pass out.

There are two Peaces. I rub my eyes to make sure I'm not seeing double, but the sight remains.

My parents never mentioned anything about Peace having a twin, unless Dr. Whisper erased another child from their memories? Then I get it. Cold dread unfurls in my chest as everything falls into place. Peace was trying to tell me there were two of him with the cutout paper brothers. One paper brother with a face, and the other without. The faceless Peace—a douen, most likely Dr. Whisper's creation. How could I not have recognized the truth when it was staring me in the face?

But which one is the real Peace? They're both strapped to chairs in gray tunics and black slacks, with two metal globes that resemble industrial-sized hair dryers above their heads.

Dr. Whisper steps out and towers over me with a blinding-white smile. "And here we are again."

My dread turns to bone-numbing fear. Happy Dr. Whisper is way more terrifying than Angry Dr. Whisper. I'm so rattled by his unnatural, wide grin, I don't notice when the Glitches move. One of them twists my wrists behind my back and another catches the camera before it hits the ground. I squeal in pain and surprise as they secure my legs and lift me into the air like a roasted pig on a stick.

I kick at one of the Glitches, but I miss, and my foot hits into a metal trolley covered with a white sheet.

"Be careful with that!" Dr. Whisper hisses, grabbing the trolley. "I'm still fixing the glitch in that model."

The sheet slides off the trolley to reveal James, his pupils white and body turned to the side. He's as still as a statue.

Nothing can stop my bloodcurdling scream. I expect Dr. Whisper to grimace in disgust, but instead he looks triumphant.

"Oh no, we're prepared for your screeching," he gloats, and raises a tong with a small silver square between it. "I infused implants into their ear canals so your obnoxiously loud voice won't upset my cocoon babies again."

"Cocoon babies?" I repeat hoarsely. The cocoons on the wall above my head bulge in acknowledgment. "I *knew* the Glitches weren't normal!"

"Normal?" Dr. Whisper chuckles. "Only unremarkable people aspire to be normal."

The Glitches tie me onto the wall next to one of the Peaces, securing my arms and feet with tubes. Then they return to their positions in front of the countdown and stare at the screen like it's the season finale of their favorite show.

Twelve minutes before midnight.

Dr. Whisper reaches for a glass jar on the top shelf with a human ear floating inside the liquid. I gasp when he uses a scalpel to slice into James's ear, but James doesn't even twitch. I can't decide if this is genius at work, madness, or a dangerous combination of the two.

With desperation, I pry at the tubes, but they're so slippery it's hard to maintain a grip. There's only one thing to do: I have to trick Dr. Whisper into a very long villain monologue while I figure out how to escape.

"You're never going to get away with this," I cry, deciding to start with a classic.

Dr. Whisper examines a shimmering silver liquid in a petri dish under a microscope. Then he pulls another beaker off the shelf and fills a syringe with a murky green liquid that is anything but kiwi Kool-Aid. All that's missing is the skull-and-crossbones sticker.

"Please don't kill me," I whisper, this time with real fear in my voice.

He looks over at me with a smile. "Oh, nothing really dies on this island. Haven't you figured it out yet?"

Jackpot.

"Should I reveal the truth?" he asks, pushing James aside. I didn't expect it would be this easy to get him talking, but he beams as if he's been waiting forever to reveal his dastardly plan.

"You see, I was committed to creating perfect children,

completely tailored to their parents' desires. Dark-haired, light-haired, blue eyes, brown eyes, but then the requests became more complex. Athletic, musically gifted"—he glares at me—"quiet."

I wince and look away.

"Do you know how hard it is to separate DNA strands? Much less if parents want their child to be smart yet don't possess intelligence themselves? How am I to identify strands that aren't there? But donors don't care about logic; they only want results."

He fills another syringe with the green liquid.

"You're insane," I reply, trying to keep him distracted. I've finally pushed a pinkie through a tight loop.

"It's true, but sane people rarely make history. For instance, after twenty years of research, they wanted to shut down my project because I failed to create their perfect children. But thanks to my *insanity*, I discovered how to make the perfect child—combining human DNA with . . . douen DNA."

I recoil with disgust. "You're sick."

"No, I'm brilliant. There are certain limitations, of course. It's hard to find compatible matches, not to mention willing douen subjects, but we've had nine successes so far, soon to be ten."

He grabs some gloves and uses one of them to point at the Peaces before sliding them onto his hands. "Peace was supposed to return once a year to prepare his brain and body for this final transformation, but no matter, it will still work." He chuckles. "Albeit more painfully."

"Did you . . ." I gulp. "Did you create the douens in the forest too?"

"I am so flattered." Dr. Whisper presses a hand to his chest and bows his head. "But I don't have the knowledge, not yet. But I did realize that instead of trying to separate DNA codes, it's easier to design the perfect child from a blank slate."

He strides over to the Peaces, the two syringes in hand. My fingers snap back into action; the tubes are starting to become loose.

"The transformation becomes permanent when the child turns six years old." He checks the timer on the wall. Five minutes until Peace's birthday. "Your real brother has been here in this lab since he arrived while the douen subject assimilated to his home life. Thanks to advanced science, we successfully transferred years of Peace's selected memories, behaviors, and emotions to the douen subject in just a few days. Our perfect Peace. There were some . . . glitches . . . but those were to be expected. You didn't have a clue."

I open my mouth to deny it, but truth is, I should have figured it out a lot sooner. Six years of memories in four days? No wonder Douen-Peace was so sluggish after the treatments. But some of those "glitches" prove that Dr. Whisper's programming isn't as exact as he believes. I'm sure he didn't mean to transfer any of Peace's affection for me to the douen, but it still broke through. I think about dinner, when his face twitched uncontrollably as I was about to drink the poisoned soup. Douen-Peace subconsciously tried to warn me.

Dr. Whisper taps a button on the wall and glass helmets lower over the Peaces' faces. A white mist fills the tube, making them look like two Peace snow globes. I'm going to lose my brother. The thought causes my palms to sweat, making it harder to escape. I claw at the tubes so hard, I rip a fingernail.

"Please, don't do this. What will happen to Peace?!"

"Oh! I almost forgot the best part. This island is magical, did you know?"

A gray sky that consumes sunlight. A forest with hardly any wildlife but douens. I would have described it as "cursed," not "magical."

"Your parents will get a douen designed to fit their needs, and the original Peace, well, anyone who dies under the age of twelve on Duppy Island turns into a douen."

"No . . ." I whisper. I don't want to believe it, but I know it must be true. My brother is going to become a douen. Peace will be a walking dead thing in three minutes, and I can't stop it.

I'm all alone here. Is this the moment in the movie when the main character realizes they have to save themselves, or is it the one where the cavalry arrives?

"Human"—he taps the Peace farther away from me—"and

douen." He taps the Peace next to me. "Douen, human." This time, he touches them in the opposite direction, so I still don't know who is the real Peace.

"And no one will know the difference." He injects a syringe into one of the metal globes, the one hovering over the Peace farther away from me, and I watch in horror as the mist in the globe turns green.

"No!" I cry out.

Dr. Whisper throws his head back and does a soft, evil laugh. I swear, I can almost see the lightning behind him.

If you ask me, that's more likely than what I actually spot in the background. The lab door opens and a slender body slides into the room, pressing himself against the wall.

Jacob!

His clothes are torn and there are cuts all over his body. His eyes are wide with fear and he's so distracted by us that he doesn't notice the Glitches behind him. I frantically signal a warning with my eyes. Thankfully the Glitches haven't noticed him either; they're still focused on the countdown.

Finally Jacob glances behind himself. Just in time. He ducks behind a table a second before one of the Glitches looks around.

Dr. Whisper watches me expectantly, waiting for my response. His eyes narrow in suspicion and he begins to turn.

"I can't believe any parent would agree to this!" I exclaim, trying to get his attention again.

It works. Dr. Whisper faces me again with a smug smile. "Even if parents agreed, do you think my donors would approve of douen-humans? Much too risky. Instead I have a way of 'changing their minds.'" He pushes down on the syringe and a tiny drop of the green liquid glistens on the tip of the needle.

My heart pounds, thinking about my parents lounging in their room, unaware of the danger. I knew he was messing with their brains, but who knows if they'll ever get their memories back? No more family dinners, movie nights, and we may never get to visit Universal Studios together. I blink away my tears; one day we may pass one another in the street like strangers.

"I know." Dr. Whisper sighs. "Such an incredible achievement and no recognition. And no one knows but you."

Jacob is very close to us now. He grabs a scalpel from another table. He's so scared his hands are shaking, and I expect the knife to fall from his grasp at any minute.

Dr. Whisper turns to check the countdown and Jacob presses himself against a file cabinet on the opposite side of the room. There's nowhere for him to hide. If Dr. Whisper shifts his gaze a millimeter to the right, he'll be exposed.

"Less than a minute to go." Dr. Whisper shivers with glee.

"No, please," I beg. The tube is looser, but there's no way I'll get my hands free in less than a minute. It's all up to Jacob now.

"Don't you want to know what happens to people who die here, once they're over twelve?" he asks.

To my surprise, Dr. Whisper draws nearer to me and leans into my face. "They turn into silver butterflies."

I barely have time to process this information, because in that moment, several things happen: The countdown clock runs out, the Glitches turn around and spot Jacob sneaking behind Dr. Whisper, and in true action-hero style, I head-butt Dr. Whisper with all my might.

He stumbles backward and drops the syringe.

"Get it!" I yell, my head throbbing with pain. The Glitches scurry toward us like lizards while Jacob dives for the syringe. He swipes it from the floor and rushes toward Dr. Whisper, who still hasn't recovered from my blow.

It's best to show the next moment in slow motion.

With the Glitches close behind him, Jacob lifts the syringe high in the air and brings it down . . . into Peace's arm.

TAKE 31—THE MIRACLE OF LIFE

Let my prolonged, terror-filled scream of "No!" echo in slow motion before focusing on the Peace next to me in real time.

Peace jerks away as far as he can in his restraints and mutters something under his breath.

"Peace! I'm here, I'm here!" I shriek.

He groans. "Serenity, why are you so loud?"

My blood grows cold. This is not my Peace.

Dr. Whisper wheels around, ready to attack, but drops his fists when he realizes it's Jacob.

And then I see the real Jacob too. The Glitches fling themselves on him in a giant embrace, like a father who's just returned home from work. His slouched back is now as straight as a rod, and he seems at least a foot taller. His eyes are narrowed in a haughty, scolding manner, and though he still looks feeble, his pale face seems more weary than sickly.

"She got you monologuing, didn't she? You're so pathetic."

Jacob sucks his teeth and throws me a backward glance, as if he expects me to join in with the ridiculing. "Sorry for the theatrics, but I couldn't resist. I wasn't lying when I said I wanted to act."

"You've got to be kidding me," I whisper. Everywhere hurts. My head, my hands, my heart. I wish I could change the channel on my life.

"What's the status on the chrysalises?" Jacob asks, batting the Glitches away. They giggle and trail after him like hungry cats.

Dr. Whisper rubs his forehead and glares at me. "There's no change in the cocoon babies—"

"For the last time, cocoons are specific to moths; *chrysalis* is the correct name for butterfly casings. And you wonder why I don't value your opinion."

Dr. Whisper doesn't answer, but the muscle in his jaw twitches.

"Have you tested the temperature?"

Dr. Whisper wriggles his fingers. It's remarkable to see this formidable man humbled by Jacob's slight frame. "Not yet. I've been preparing Peace for the final transfer—"

"Peace isn't important," Jacob snaps, and both Dr. Whisper and I flinch.

"Rude," Douen-Peace says in a slurred voice. "Am I fully human yet?"

Jacob ignores him. "He's the last in a defunct, outdated

program when we had to pair douens and humans. The chrysalis babies are the future of Your Perfect Child." He lifts his chin with pride.

"I just need to check the vitals on—"

"Go." Jacob doesn't raise his voice, but the authority in his tone is louder than any yell.

Dr. Whisper presses his lips together in a thin line and then walks over to the area with the cocoons in a slow, deliberate manner, like an unwilling child. He passes my camera, which is on a table facing the Glitches, and the red light blinks. It still has charge! And perhaps has been recording this entire time.

"Good help is so hard to find." Jacob puts the empty syringe on the trolley next to James, not taking a second glance at his brother. Then he releases a heavy sigh. "I wish you had stayed out of the clinic, Serenity."

I keep waiting for a wink, or some other sign that this is all part of an elaborate act to save me. Or maybe Dr. Whisper is messing with my head in some sick game. Maybe he did something to Jacob when he treated him for his asthma attack.

As if he read my mind, Jacob rolls his eyes. "Do you really think that buffoon is still behind it all? Serenity, it was me"—he gestures around the lab—"I'm the douen who saved his program."

At this point, I'm so emotionally exhausted my shock

comes out as a sigh. Jacob could have changed his face like a dirty T-shirt and I would have just shrugged. He seems disappointed by my lukewarm reaction.

"If you're gonna take your face off, can you change into Jackie Opel?" I ask in a deflated tone.

Jacob's face drops—in the metaphorical way. Not literally. "I thought you liked my face?"

"That was before I saw the real person behind it."

Our eyes meet and after a few seconds, I break the gaze.

Then I notice the scalpel on the ground, close to my feet. I wiggle my hand. Another finger pops out and hits against a hard piece of plastic in my back pocket. I had forgotten all about my camera trigger!

A light bulb goes off in my head and a jolt of hope runs through me. *This* is the moment when the character realizes she can save everyone.

Jacob gives me a small smile. "Fun fact. Did you know 'Why?' is the last question on most people's lips before they die?"

I shake my head. "You want your chance to monologue too, huh?"

He chuckles and then grows somber. "I prefer to use visuals."

Jacob moves to a short filing cabinet and pulls the cover off a square frame. It's a fish tank, except inside are a handful of silver butterflies.

I gasp in surprise and so does Douen-Peace. The Glitches gather around the tank, intrigued.

"What are you doing with those butterflies?" Douen-Peace demands. His voice is louder than usual. Maybe fifty-five decibels.

The butterflies desperately flutter inside the tank. I don't need to hear their score to know they're afraid. I look across at the shimmering liquid in the petri dish and back to the butterflies, and my stomach churns.

"Douens need these silver butterflies to survive. We can't live anywhere else but on Duppy Island. You know what happened when I tried to leave."

I am confused, until he chooses that moment to cough and it hits me. He's the boy from the Captain's story! I'm so stunned I forget I'm trying to escape. That would make him, like, over two hundred years old?

Gross.

"I realized no one was coming to save me, and I swore never to depend on anything ever again. I dedicated my life to finding a way to sever the butterfly connection for all douens, and now, I've finally succeeded."

He puts his hand on the glass, but his presence is like a repellent. All the butterflies flutter to the opposite corner of the tank. "Sometimes I miss them."

"I don't get it. How did you do it?" I ask, and I genuinely want to know, not just to buy time.

"It wasn't easy. When Dr. Whisper first came, the original douens—the red ones—weren't happy. The construction caused a lot of butterfly deaths, but I'm the only one who saw it as an opportunity. I'd sneak into the lab to experiment on myself. Nothing had exceptional results until I started to experiment with butterfly DNA."

Douen-Peace and I gasp again. "They're endangered," I whisper, repulsed.

Jacob's eyes flash in anger. "It's for the greater good! Now douens have a chance for a perfect family. Something I never got to experience! Everyone deserves a happy family. Everyone."

We stare down each other again, his eyes begging me to understand and mine full of disgust.

"The chrysalis babies are the future—we fixed all the glitches."

The Glitches turn and wave at the sound of their name, then continue to gaze at the butterflies. I pray they don't shift the camera.

"No need for human swaps, no need to wait six years. And it's so tedious to erase and transfer memories."

"I didn't agree to this," Douen-Peace says, his voice breaking. "You never said anything about hurting butterflies or losing memories."

"It's too late," Jacob says. "The final transformation is already taking place. Don't worry, it's for your own good. You'll soon have a happy home, and you won't remember any of this."

Douen-Peace struggles against the restraints. "I changed my mind. I don't want to." He turns to me, his eyes wide with fear, and though I know he's not the real Peace, my heart still breaks. "Help . . ."

His voice trails away and his head drops. Next to him, the real Peace starts to shake and his nose begins to shrink. I scratch at my pocket to get out the trigger, twisting my hand with more urgency. I hope there's still time to save him.

Then I understand what Trill meant when he said butterflies are life.

"B-but," I stutter, "if you kill the butterflies, you're killing the douens; you're killing your own people."

Jacob sighs. "It's so hard to be a visionary. The red douens don't understand either, but it's not their fault. They don't know any better. They kept storming the facility, so we had to install the lights and frequency blocker. You saw how they treated me in the forest. That panic was real. I barely escaped."

Trill begged me to kill the lights but I didn't listen. Suddenly it's clear what I have to do; I only hope it's not too late for Peace. My hands are almost free.

"So James and John aren't your brothers, then?"

Jacob smiles. "No, more experimental chrysalis babies."

"And Uncle Newton isn't really your dad?"

There's a flicker of emotion on his face. "Newton is this boy's father—the owner of this face. Newton was a fisherman and got into some difficulty at sea with his son. It was too late to save the boy, but his DNA allowed me to perfect the formula to merge humans and douens. He died the day after his twelfth birthday, and on that day, I left my birth name behind—Elijah."

I shake my head in disbelief as I remember the engraving in the cherry-tree clearing and understand it was Jacob's old resting place. Trill tried to warn me. Why didn't I listen?

He coughs again, the sound rattling in his chest, and then clears his throat. "I severed my connection to the butterflies before I figured out the right sequence, so I have to live with the side effects. That asthma attack was real too, by the way. Thanks for saving me."

"You're welcome. Any chance you'll return the favor and let me go?"

He smirks and then gives me an intense look. "You could stay here with me, you know. And Peace. You can train him to be the perfect brother. Let your parents leave with their perfect son. Trust me, they won't miss you. It's a win for everyone."

I return a cold look. "You can't force people into who you want them to be, Jacob. You have to love them for who they are."

Jacob's face twists and he looks at me with such disgust that I immediately recognize him as the shadowed figure in my nightmare. "It really was you all along."

He shrugs. "Who would have thought I'd become friends with that loud brat? You may not remember, but you walked in on the birth of the Glitches six years ago."

He glances at the cocoons on the wall. The one on the left looks like it's having a boxing match with the casing. "Isn't it funny how life works?"

Dr. Whisper calls from across the room. "It's ready."

Tears of frustration stream down my face. Peace's nose is completely gone now and his right eye is missing. Jacob spins on his heels with delight. "Cue the evil mad-scientist laugh!"

The Glitches form a semicircle around the cocoon and start to snap their fingers in applause.

The cocoon begins to vibrate. Then the silver dots sink into the casing, and it gets more and more transparent until we see a baby pressed against the flimsy wall. I watch in morbid fascination as a face appears on the baby, slowly twisting into place like the time lapse of a sculpture.

If I were to score this scene, I'd use quick, low drumbeats with Jacob's mad-scientist laugh in the background. Cue some thunder and lightning for added effect.

A tiny hand bursts through the sack.

I've got the trigger! I press down on the button, praying there's enough charge left in the camera. At first, nothing happens, but then there's a small click, and a second later, a bright flash.

The Glitches recoil in surprise and crash into the table,

knocking down beakers, test tubes, and the glass cage with the butterflies.

Jacob and Dr. Whisper cry out and rush to save whatever's left of their research. It's the distraction I needed. I free my hands and lunge for the scalpel.

"Stop her!" Jacob yells. The Glitches are still disoriented, but they stumble toward me.

Please let this work. Please let this work.

I yank a plug out of a nearby socket and use the scalpel to slice through the plastic covering and into the wires inside. Then, just as the Glitches are closing in, I shove the damaged cord back into the socket.

There is a short sizzle, a loud pop, and the entire room goes dark.

Almost immediately after, music fills the air.

TAKE 32—HAPPY BIRTHDAY

Another glass of something crashes onto the floor, and Dr. Whisper releases a string of words that should be bleeped out if you want to keep the film suitable for kids.

"Stay still!" Dr. Whisper cries. "The backup generator should kick in any minute now."

"It's too late." Jacob's solemn voice cuts through the darkness. "They're already here."

I'm still disoriented by the sudden flood of music around me, dominated by Dr. Whisper's terrible sound that I first heard when I arrived on Duppy Island.

Wait, no, the never-ending cry of loss has to be Jacob!

I will not feel sorry for the person about to kill me. I will not feel sorry for the person about to kill me. I will not.

Dr. Whisper's music is the grating sound I heard before in the prison. It's still unpleasant, though not as bad as Jacob's. It reminds me of a shopping cart with a wobbly wheel moving across pavement.

Then, there it is. The sound of a paintbrush—getting

238

fainter and fainter by the second. I get on all fours and crawl toward the noise, trying my best to block out Jacob and praying that I don't bump into any of the Glitches.

But it's hard to keep track of Peace's music. And the only light comes from the blinking zeros from the countdown that are only strong enough to illuminate the HAPPY BIRTH-DAY sign below it. It feels like I'm in a wild dance party with five deejays blasting different tunes.

Then the cavalry arrives.

Trill's cowboy whistle cuts through the pandemonium. I crawl toward the sound and find two bodies that both emit fading brushstroke music. It was impossible to tell who was the real Peace when it was well-lit. How on earth am I to know the difference in darkness?

I make a weak attempt to lift both of them at the same time.

A rough hand closes over mine, and I immediately know it is Trill. Again, his presence calms my nerves. He takes one of the Peaces from me, and after I lift the second Peace over my shoulder, I grab on to his arm. He leads us through the melee and out the door.

Inside, the clinic is pitch-black as well. Even with Trill's guidance, I still accidentally bump into the rough walls, but I keep up the pace. I need to get my parents; find a way to save the real Peace; somehow avoid superhuman six-year-olds, an ancient human-douen mutation, and an unstable genetics scientist; and make it to the jetty in time to meet the Captain at sunrise.

I'm able to check the second item off my list when we burst through the clinic doors and run smack-dab into my flustered parents.

Without the artificial lights beaming from the rooftop, you can see the clear sky, and the courtyard is bathed in moonlight. The silence of the facility is gone; I can hear the sounds of the trees, the leaves, the air, and most importantly, the pitter-patter of my parents' music.

"Mum! Dad!" I exclaim in relief, before remembering they have no idea who I am.

"Peace!" They both reach for him, but Mum gets there first. She grabs Peace and swings him away from me, as if I'm the one who put him in danger.

I know they're not themselves, but it still hurts seeing my own parents be wary of me. Their distrust breaks me in two.

Then their expressions immediately change to shock when Trill steps into the moonlight. Mum lets out something between a scream and the sound effect you use for a scary cartoon ghost. Forgive her—this is the loudest sound she's made in years; her throat is a little rusty. Plus, it's a lot to take in.

One: There's a boy with no face in a mushroom hat. Two: There's a second Peace over his shoulder, who is missing an eye and a nose. And three: There's a tiny brown baby in the crook of his arm. The cocoon baby grabs at the air and its face twists into an empty wail.

"Oh my God." Dad studies Trill with fear and fascination. He glances at the Peace on his shoulder, then back over to Mum's Peace. You can practically hear the cogs in his brain trying to make sense of the situation. He takes a step toward Trill cautiously, like he's approaching a wild animal. Trill, to my surprise, smiles at Dad and comes forward to meet him. He gently puts the sleeping Peace Two in his arms.

Dad backs away, eyes still roving over Trill. "I can't believe it. Douens are real?"

"Adisa," Mum says, pulling him away. "There are two Peaces. Focus on that. What the hell is going on?"

Trill taps me and gestures at my parents, but I don't have the time or patience to read his lips. My nervous parents take a few more steps away from us, toward the clinic.

"Mum, I can explain, but—"

"Child, we are not your parents." She might as well have slapped me in the face. It's not their fault, yet it still stings that they don't recognize me.

"Where's Dr. Whisper? He can explain this," Dad says, more to himself than anyone else. They move toward the clinic but I block their way. I can't let them put themselves in more danger.

"Dad, your worst fear is that your first book will go out

of print—you bought two hundred copies for archival purposes. I can't ever tell the difference between your white linen shirts, but your favorite one has a tiny brown stain by the pocket. Mum, your most popular ASMR video is you rolling a Q-tip in a mannequin's ear, but your personal favorite is the one where you rub your makeup brush and hairbrush together. It's the only one saved on your desktop. And when you guys think no one's looking, you—ugh—bump noses in the kitchen to say I love you."

Dad and Mum gawk at me, open-mouthed. Maybe a single violin note would be fitting at this moment, because I started to cry during my speech.

I wipe away my tears. "I can explain everything, but we're all in trouble right now. You think you don't know me, but you're my parents and I love you, and I need you to trust me."

They do their silent communication, look at the two Peaces, and then nod.

I turn to Trill. "Take us to the safe place."

He doesn't seem happy, but he leads us to the back of the clinic to enter the forest.

"I'm not sure about this," Dad says when we get near the edge of the fence. "Maybe we should—"

But he doesn't get a chance to finish.

Trill stops dead in the path, and then I hear it too. The melody of wind in the trees is so strong it sounds like a hurricane moving through the branches. The sky brightens up ahead, and it's not from the full moon but a swarm of butterflies crowding the sky.

They are like a plague of silver locusts. I've never seen anything so beautiful, until the meaning of the swarm hits me.

Butterflies are life, and where there are butterflies, there are douens.

There's nothing to stop them from storming the facility . . . and the red douens don't know the good humans from the bad ones.

Trill turns to me, echoing my name, but his mouth forms one word over and over again:

Run.

TAKE 33—WELCOME BACK

A second later, the sound of the wind turns into whispering—nothing that anyone can understand, but the anger in the words is so unquestionable I don't have to tell my parents to run.

We dash back into the courtyard in time to see Dr. Whisper, Jacob, and the Glitches piling into the airship. Uncle Newton is close behind with Timoteeth in his arms.

"Wait!" I cry, but Mum and Dad ignore me and hurry to the airship, so I have no choice but to follow. Trill grabs at my hand to stop me, but I wrench it away.

There's nowhere to hide—every direction spells death—so if I have to die, I want to be with my family.

Just as Uncle Newton is getting inside the airship, Timoteeth hops out of his arms and bounds toward the bathroom stalls. Uncle Newton jumps off the steps and follows the bunny.

Jacob pushes his head out the door. "Forget the rabbit,

you idiot!" he cries, but Uncle Newton ignores him. Jacob notices us coming and his face twists with rage. And then his eyes widen with fright. "Dad!" he yells, in a desperate, high-pitched voice.

I turn around and the sight causes my stomach to drop to my toes.

A crowd of red douens, at least three times the number I saw earlier in the forest, pour into the courtyard like a pack of hyenas chasing a stampede of gazelles. Except there is no pummeling of hooves; the silence makes it all the scarier.

If I were scoring this scene, I'd lightly brush my fingertips on top of a mic to capture the sound of backward feet on the tiles.

When I turn around, Jacob is chasing after Uncle Newton and the bunny. Dr. Whisper pushes half his body outside, grabbing the door handle. He smirks at us and then slams the door shut, just as we are about to climb the stairs. My parents bang on the closed door, and a few seconds later, the propellers begin to turn.

I check to see if the douens are on our heels, but to my relief, they're all converged around the clinic. Some of them storm inside, crashing through the glass doors like they were made out of biscuit. Others scurry up the side of the building like giant spiders, toward the lights.

The backup generator has kicked in and the lights are

booting up, a warm glow coming from their centers, but it's way too late.

I gasp as the first light comes tumbling down from the roof. I cover my ears and try to warn my parents, but they slam their hands onto their ears a second too late. If the noise was painful for me, it must be excruciating for them. And also the douens. For a moment, everything stands still as everyone—both human and douen—grimaces in pain.

Then I notice Trill waving at me from in front of the house with the blacked-out windows. Not a moment too soon. A pair of douens jump down from the roof, landing in poses fit for the latest superhero movie, and snap their heads in our direction.

"This way!" I shout to my parents. The Peace in Dad's arms shifts his head, but there's no time to celebrate or interrogate him. We're next on the douens' radar and they seem as strong as Thor and his hammer combined. Together we race toward Trill, who holds the door open for us. Then there's a loud explosion behind me.

I wheel around to see smoke billowing from the clinic's doors. A small figure in a gray tunic bursts through the smoke. It's James!

He vanishes in the space between the clinic and the warren. Then the roof of the building explodes like the top of a volcano. The airship still hadn't cleared the clinic. I watch as it swerves to avoid the smoke and disappear into the trees, right before Trill yanks me into the house.

Inside, I grab the crank radio from my bag and put it on the lowest setting, hoping the light won't hurt Trill. I point it at his feet and he opens the hatch.

"We're going down there?" Mum asks in an incredulous voice. "Is it safe?"

"Safer than up here," Dad answers.

In the cell, Trill runs his fingers along the walls, and though his back is turned, he frantically gestures for me to move the light away.

"This is remarkable," Dad says in awe. "I read about this quarantine facility, but I can't believe the cells are still here."

"I know, I know, for cholera cases in 1854, blah blah," I reply, nipping his lecture in the bud. "How is Peace?" I shine the light on Dad, who is on the ground checking Peace's temperature with the back of his hand.

"Is he okay?" I ask, shining the light on his face.

His face! He has a full face. That's a good sign! But then there's a chorus of whispering from above.

"They're here." I put the flashlight on the floor, pointing it toward the cell bars, and then rush to help Trill.

I assume we're searching for some secret door. I pat all the bricks on the wall, but Trill puts his palm on top of mine, then brings my hand to his ear.

Listen.

I get it now. If I remember correctly, I heard his music in the corner by the bed frame. I pull him to the area, and sure enough, the air feels lighter in that spot.

Bam! Trill slams his fist into the wall.

I gasp and try to stop him, but he slams it into the brick again.

A crack appears in the wall. Trill folds his lips and keeps smashing into the wall. One of the bricks finally cracks and dirt falls onto the floor.

Trill plunges his hand into the broken wall and exhales like he downed a glass of ice water on a hot day. He pulls his arm out, bringing a tangle of leaves and branches in his fist, and a sliver of moonlight penetrates the darkness.

It's a way out.

The whispering gets louder above us, and this time the words are clear.

Hurt. Hurt. Hurt.

Trill punches the wall again, and though it makes another crack, there's no way he's going to create a hole big enough for us all to fit through before the douens arrive.

Then, bam! Another hole appears in the wall. This one made by Mum's Peace.

Mum, Dad, and I gape at Peace helping Trill punch through the wall like a tiny superhero. I imagine this is how Lois Lane felt when she realized Clark Kent was Superman.

Dad moves closer to Mum and puts an arm over her shoulder while stroking the other Peace's head. That must be the real Peace . . . I hope.

With twice the manpower, soon there's a hole big enough for us to escape.

Trill and Douen-Peace shove more bricks away and we squeeze through the hole, one after the other, and push through the forest.

TAKE 34—FAMILY REUNION

Ever wondered how it would feel to get lost in a bowl of potpourri? Well, now I can tell you. We eat leaves, branches, and some surprisingly sweet-tasting vines for what seems to be an eternity.

Trill and Douen-Peace slip through the trees like oil on a silver spoon, while my parents and I fight to get through the tight spaces.

I keep checking to make sure my parents and Peace are behind me, but in the bush they're shadows in the dark. So I focus on their music instead. Peace's brushstrokes are getting stronger, to my relief, but if he's awake he hasn't said a word. That's pretty normal, but I'm worried about potential side effects from Jacob's serum.

Did the experiment fail? Did I interrupt it in time? If we make it back to the port, will Peace's face disappear in the taxi? Douen-Peace's score has changed to a sad, dragging brushstroke, so miserable that I *almost* forgive him for the past week.

Finally the trees and bush start to thin out, and we enter a space wide enough for us to stretch our bruised arms and legs.

Dad, still carrying Peace, opens his mouth to talk, but I shush him.

I gotta say, it feels good to do that.

I gesture that it's not safe to speak yet, and it's a good thing I do.

Moments later, there is giggling in the air.

Trill, Douen-Peace, and I move to hide in the bushes, and it's only when a confused Mum and Dad follow our lead that I realize they can't hear the sound.

The giggling is someone's music, and it doesn't belong to one person, but two.

James and John skip through the clearing, throwing leaves up into the air and attempting to catch them as they fall.

Neither of them have faces but they don't seem to care now that they're together again. We all stay quiet until they're out of sight.

I exhale with relief when we make it to the cherry clearing. The area feels different, like an empty room, and I realize there are no butterflies around. Without them, the space is depressing, even though it's lit by the moonlight.

Trill guides Douen-Peace over to the mounds, scoops up handfuls of dirt, and sprinkles it over his bowed head. Dad rests Peace on the ground under a large tree before collapsing by his feet. Mum sits next to Dad, crosses her legs, and starts to meditate.

As I catch my breath, my mind rehashes the events of the last couple of hours.

I did it. I survived a near-inescapable situation. There're only two items left on my checklist: save the real Peace and get to the jetty by sunrise.

I join my parents under the tree. They may not recognize me as their daughter, but being close to them still brings me comfort.

A deep cut on the back of my hand burns, so I bury my fingers in the soil, just like I did last time. It's like I dunked my skin into soothing, mint-scented cream.

This island really is magical.

"My brain is out of alignment," Mum says, rubbing her temples. "I can't get a clear picture of anything."

"Serenity, right?" Dad asks, without opening his eyes. "Please explain everything that just happened, in clear sentences, please."

Dad's rain is thundering down in an erratic manner, as if the wind is blowing the drops every direction. His voice is calm, but my dad is scared.

Mum rests a hand on his shoulder and some of the thunder disappears, just like that. Then she turns to me and reaches into her pocket. "I know you, but I don't understand how."

She opens her fist to reveal a crumpled paper person—
Peace's cutout of me.

My voice catches in a sob and I take deep breaths to pull
myself together, but too much of me is breaking apart. Mum
extends her arms and I waste no time hopping into them.

I hide my face in her sweaty dashiki, a flood of tears running down my cheeks.

Then Mum stiffens. Trill is coming toward us.

Dad jumps up—well, he gets to his feet as quickly as a
person who's trekked through the forest for hours can. He
takes the stance of someone who has never been in an actual
fistfight in their life.

"It's okay, he's my friend."

Dad drops his fists, but he's still tense.

Trill stops a few feet away from us, and he and Dad look
each other over. I'm about to break the silence when Dad
scratches his chin.

"This is actually remarkable," he says, still taking in Trill's
appearance. "I can't believe the rumors are true. This is a
monumental discovery—does anyone have a pen?"

Trill smiles and opens his mouth. *Serenity.*

Dad jumps and tries to stop me from moving closer, but I
wave his hand away. "He won't hurt me."

I have to squint to read Trill's lips in the moonlight.
These will help.

He points to me, Dad, and Mum, and puts three cherries

into my hand. They're extremely plump and ready to burst with juice . . . and into song. Their harmonies reverberate like Mum's Tibetan singing bowls.

I bring one to my mouth, anxious to taste their sweetness, but then I pause and take the cherries over to my parents; we should do this together, as a family. We hesitate for a second before popping the cherries into our mouths.

And then the world explodes. I am bowled over by memories as soon as the juice and melody touch my tongue.

If I were to score this scene, I'd have that rewind sound effect while the major events in my life replay backward, slowing down at key moments: when I arrived on Duppy Island, Mum and Dad presenting me with my camera on Christmas Day, the night I first had my nightmare, until we get to that moment when I first visited the clinic six years ago.

Six-year-old me screams as the faceless Glitches crawl out of their cocoons. A much healthier-looking Jacob stares down at me in disgust and raises the syringe in his hand.

"Serenity!" Mum's hug knocks the wind out of my chest. She buries her face in my hair. "I'm so sorry, my darling girl, I'm so sorry."

I feel the weight of Dad's arms.

"Welcome back." My voice is muffled in her clothes.

Mum raises her head. "What about Peace?"

Douen-Peace steps in front of my parents with a coconut

husk of water and waits for permission to come closer. His eyes and nose have now vanished after Trill's ritual by the mounds, but he still radiates Peace's essence.

After my parents nod, Douen-Peace puts the husk to Peace's lips. At first, nothing happens, but then Peace grabs on to the shell and chugs the water. I hold my breath, waiting to see which Peace will emerge.

He sits up and surveys the area, taking in the trees, the douens, gazing at Mum and Dad, and then finally, his eyes linger on me. We stare at each other, neither of us wanting to say the first word, and my eyes fill up with tears. In that moment, I realize it doesn't matter which Peace he chooses to be. My brother is alive and I'll love him no matter which personality he takes.

He gives his slight half smile. "I knew you'd save me, Ren."

And then he's in my arms. I don't know which of us moved first, but I hold on to him and pour all the mushy feelings I've never said out loud into that hug.

"I'm sorry, I'm sorry, I'm sorry," Peace repeats.

I pull away and place my hands on his shoulders. "You have nothing to be sorry for. You've been so brave."

I hug him again. "Happy birthday, Ace," I whisper in his ear. Okay, this is another cliché, but nothing can depict the emotion in this reunion better than a string of violins.

My parents join in on the Noah family group hug. As

though it was kismet, a few butterflies return and flutter above our heads, casting a brighter light in the area.

"It didn't work," I say to my parents. "Dr. Whisper said the treatment becomes permanent on his sixth birthday. He had the countdown set to midnight and everything."

"Peace was born at seven minutes past twelve, not twelve o'clock," Mum clarifies.

An oversight on Dr. Whisper's part! Jacob would be furious. Peace was a mere seven minutes away from death.

"I still don't know how everything happened? How could we—" Mum looks at Dad with the question in her eyes.

"Dr. Whisper altered your memories," I reply.

I recap all the events from the moment I arrived on Duppy Island.

My parents are the perfect audience, gasping at all the right moments—when Peace's feet turned backward (they check to see if they're front-facing) and when the Glitches lost their faces.

But when I get to the events in the lab, their eyes harden. They're no longer surprised by the mutant bunnies, the cocoons, or the fact that Jacob was a douen.

When I'm done, there's a long silence.

Mum finally responds with urgency in her voice. "You have to believe us, Serenity. We would have never allowed him to do this. We were supposed to come back here every year for monitoring, but we never did. And it wasn't just the money. I had a terrible feeling about this place, but I couldn't figure out why. It's only when Peace had the panic attack and started seeing shadows that we—"

Her voice cracks. Dad hurries over to comfort her, but Mum wheels away in anger.

"We weren't even expecting his treatment to work! But what was the harm? Why not try to give our baby qualities and skills that could give them a leg up in life?"

"It's okay," I reassure them. "Dr. Whisper brainwashed you."

"He did later on, yes," Dad replies. "But we joined the program in the first place. That's on us. He didn't make us do that, and we'll never forgive ourselves."

Both my parents drop their heads in shame.

My throat is so dry it hurts to swallow. Trill passes over a husk full of coconut water. The drink sweeps away the fatigue and replaces it with pure energy.

"Is everything here magic?" I ask, but Trill just smiles and cracks open another coconut.

Dad shifts his foot and takes up a piece of caked mud. He scrapes the soil away to reveal a square object. It looks like an antique brass stamp.

"Oh, my word, could it be . . ." he whispers.

Trill drops the coconut husks and backs away. His score becomes frantic.

"What is it?" I ask Trill, but Dad answers.

"It's a scarificator. They used these in the nineteenth century to bleed patients." Dad presses down on a button and tiny blades snap out. "Back then, they thought removing bad blood could cure certain diseases."

He digs his foot into the dirt again and it slides on some kind of woven sack. He plucks a coin from the soil and scratches the mud away.

"A half penny! From 1854. You know what? This may be a gravesite for people who were sent here during the cholera pandemic." Dad grabs a stick and prods into different parts of the soil.

"That's how Jacob died!" I exclaim, and turn to Trill, who is now hiding behind a cherry tree. "And you too, Trill?" I ask. "You died in the 1850s from cholera?"

"Trill?"

Dad is focused on Trill, his eyes wide and lips trembling. "As in O'Brien Trill Cumberbatch?"

Trill jumps from behind the tree and claps his hands. Then he twirls and wiggles his fingers like Peace and I do when we sing "fantabulosome." Trill echoes the name "O'Brien," but his lips repeat the phrase: *You know me.*

Dad drops the stick. "Nah, it can't be . . ."

"How did you know Trill's name?" I ask, my gaze switching between the two of them.

Dad is shell-shocked, looking at the dirty coin and then back at Trill. I tug on his hand to break him out of his trance.

"Serenity," he gasps in a tiny voice. "Th-this douen . . . might be my great-great-great"—Dad's smile gets bigger every time he says the word—"great-great-uncle."

TAKE 35—TASTE THE RAINBOW

Now, I know you expect me to suggest a really dramatic score here, maybe the "tum tum tum tum tummmmmmm" filmmakers use when there's a reveal as surprising as this one.

But instead, I recommend the clink of glasses—the sound of all the pieces falling into place—because as soon as the words left Dad's lips, I had no doubt it was the truth.

I always felt a strange connection to Trill: It makes sense that he's family.

"Adisa, he's just a child," Mum says in a gentle voice.

"He was young when he died, remember? Children who die here turn into douens," I remind her. Mum sighs and presses a hand against her chest.

"He's the musician! The prodigy!" Dad squeals, tapping Mum on the shoulder. "Used to make music from everything: pumpkin vines, bamboo pipes—a one-man percussion band. I found his name on a bill of entertainment."

Trill takes Dad's hand and leads him to the mounds. Dad turns to us and mouths *oh my God*, and I can't help but grin. He's as excited as a tween at their favorite celebrity's concert.

Douen-Peace comes up to Peace, rocking the cocoon baby in his arms. It still hasn't made a sound. I hope it's alive.

"Forgive," Douen-Peace echoes.

I stay quiet. While I'm grateful he helped us escape, I haven't forgotten he also tried to poison me.

Peace offers Douen-Peace some of the coconut water and even puts a few drops into the cocoon baby's mouth. Trust Peace to forgive the person who tried to steal his life and memories without a second thought. I'm pretty sure he has a silver butterfly living in his heart.

"Everybody," Dad calls, and we head over to the mounds.

Dad displays the items in his hand. The clearing is a treasure trove of goodies for a historian. He found a clay pipe, pieces of pottery and crocus bags, and a few more coins.

"These are unmarked graves. The final resting place for so many people, including children, who were shipped off to this island for quarantine."

Dad pulls across a few of the vines and there is silence as we survey the hundreds of mounds. I hate that there's nothing here to honor their memory, to acknowledge that so many people suffered and died on this island.

Then I remember the brass cross in the reception desk.

"Would a pastor have blessed this area?" I ask.

Dad nods. "Most likely."

"Maybe that's why the red douens stay away. We can stay here until sunrise and then head to the jetty. That's when they go to sleep, right, Trill?"

He nods.

Dad checks his watch. "That's two hours away. Are you *sure* we're safe here?"

Trill nods again and mouths: *Safe place.*

I translate for my parents and Mum furrows her eyebrows. "You understand him?"

"We have a special connection," I reply, winking at Trill. I'm not ready to share my lipreading skill yet. For now, it'll be a special secret between me and Trill. My parents don't question me further, but from their expressions, it's clear the conversation isn't over.

"Serenity, maybe you can translate for me. I have so many questions," Dad says, patting his pockets. "Ask him his sister's name, and his mother!"

Trill sits on a mound and starts to mouth words to me. It takes a while, but I finally decipher my ancestors' names to help Dad reconnect our broken lineage.

Mum observes Peace while he rocks the cocoon baby in his arms. It's definitely alive; when Douen-Peace leans over to brush something from its face, it reaches up to tug at one of the palms in his mushroom hat.

"We need to expose Dr. Whisper and his corrupt program," Mum says with steel in her voice.

"But we haven't got proof," I reply, and then Trill raises his hand. He swings the coconut-palm leaves around his waist and lifts up one of the palms. I'm about to cover my eyes when I see my camera tied to the leaves, along with my iPod. Trill is the best!

"You can keep it," I tell him as he tries to hand over the iPod . . .

"I'll take everything, thank you."

Dr. Whisper steps into the clearing. His white coat is laced with muddy stains and covered in vegetation, everywhere except his face. Even the leaves are too repulsed to touch it. His grinding music fluctuates as he wavers between staying calm and exploding with anger. After seeing Jacob belittle him in the lab, my mind-numbing fear is gone and I see him for what he is: a desperate, greedy man.

"You!" Mum cries, but luckily Dad is able to stop her from attacking.

The Glitches pop up behind Dr. Whisper and form a circle around us. However, instead of focusing on us, their eyes wander around the area. One of them sniffs at the cherry tree. They've never stepped foot off the facility before; this must seem like a whole new country to them.

Dr. Whisper has to snap his fingers to get their attention. "Get the camera and the cocoon baby."

I had hoped that, like the red douens, they wouldn't be able to come into the clearing, but the Glitches enter without any trouble.

Dad, Mum, Trill, and Douen-Peace step in front of us. Dad holds his stick out like a bat and looks over his shoulder. "Run," he says to me. "Take care of your brother."

I grab Peace's free hand and we scamper toward the darkest part of the forest, him clutching the cocoon baby to his chest. I take a quick glance at Dr. Whisper, who is now chasing after us from above the clearing.

I push Peace under a rocky ledge, but instead of joining him, I use a prickly vine to hide him and the baby.

"I'll be back," I promise him, and head in the opposite direction, toward a thick cluster of trees, making sure Dr. Whisper sees me before I duck between them.

I press against a tree, listening for Dr. Whisper's music. Peace will be safe as long as he's focused on me. I also have a full view of the clearing from my hiding spot, so I use the last bit of camera charge to film the scene.

The Glitches close in on everyone, swatting away the sticks and stones hurled at them as if they were made of paper.

But then, Trill pelts some cherries at the Glitches with amazing, zippy accuracy. The fruits burst on the spots above their lips and the juice trickles into their mouths.

If they were cartoons, their eyes would have bulged out of their heads, and they would have floated into the air in bliss. The Glitches release little squeals of delight and run their tongues over their lips, trying to capture every drop of their first taste of fresh fruit. They drop to the ground and push the smashed berries into their mouths.

I hear their new melody. It is a crackling sound, like bread-fruit roasting on an open fire. As I expect, when they look up their faces are gone. The small silver ear implants drop out of their ears.

They've returned to their roots.

Mum and Dad both yelp; I can't blame them. You never get accustomed to it. But their loud cries cause the Glitches to flinch and hiss at them. My camera dies as Trill is gesturing for them to be quiet.

That's when I realize Dr. Whisper's grating music is farther away from me, and closer to Peace.

I pop out from the bush, just when Dr. Whisper is about to discover Peace's hiding spot.

"Looking for this?" I lift the camera in the air.

Dr. Whisper's face is murderous as he marches toward me. I slip between the trees, at times just avoiding his grasp, until the forest becomes sparse and I face another curtain of vines.

"Nowhere left to hide now," Dr. Whisper says, his face sweaty and breathing hard.

I back into the burial ground, taking my eyes off him for a split second to glance behind myself.

"It's over," I say, gripping the camera. "Why don't you run while you still have the chance?"

A handful of silver butterflies fly down from the trees and hover above us.

"Look, I'm a reasonable man," Dr. Whisper replies, placing his hands behind his back. "Just give me the camera and I'll leave. I won't hurt you. I promise."

But his music says otherwise. It's escalating instead of becoming more subdued. One of the silver butterflies drifts below his arm, its glow revealing the tip of a syringe in his hand.

I put the camera on the ground in front of me. "Then come and get it."

Dr. Whisper's mouth curls, but then he forces it into a smile and advances slowly.

When he bends down to get the camera, his grating music snaps. I jump out of the way a split second before he lunges at me with the syringe. Dr. Whisper yelps and releases another censored word as he topples into Elijah's/Jacob's open grave.

There's a loud thud and a second later, the shouting begins. So loud he could wake the dead. I grab the camera and scramble away in case he manages to climb out.

But Dr. Whisper doesn't get the chance.

Five faceless figures in gray tunics burst through the vines, their fingers pointed ahead . . . at me. I cower and protect my face as the Glitches scurry toward me, their mouths twisted in pain, but they swerve at the last second and jump into the grave.

And then Dr. Whisper stops screaming.

His grating music gets softer and softer until it disappears.

I run through the vines, meeting my parents, Trill and Douen-Peace racing toward me on the other side.

"Serenity," Trill echoes. And I don't have to read his lips to understand. The clearing is no longer safe.

I tell them what happened to Dr. Whisper as we get Peace and the cocoon baby from their hiding place. Trill stares at Douen-Peace, communicating in a way only douens under-stand. Douen-Peace nods and puts the cocoon baby over his shoulder. Then he bows to Peace and gives the rest of us a soldier's salute before running in the opposite direction of the Glitches.

"We have to go to the beach now," I tell my parents.

"What about the red douens—it's an hour before sunrise. They may still be awake," Dad says.

"We don't have a choice," I whisper, glancing at the vines. The Glitches could return at any moment.

Hand in hand, we follow Trill through a forest filled with douens eager to rip us apart. Still, if I had to score this scene, I'd use an upbeat adventure tune, similar to the ones in superhero movies. Because finally, the Noahs are reunited and ready to face the next challenge together, as a family.

TAKE 36—NAAMAH'S CHOICE

I take it back.

We are not superheroes.

Superheroes don't whisper-complain every time their hair catches on a wayward branch (Mum) or pause to examine every leaf for its properties (Dad). Seriously if we had capes, Mum would use hers to wipe away sweat, and then Dad would use his as a notepad. Meanwhile, we would all have to keep an eye on Peace, who would absentmindedly follow every silver butterfly that flutters by.

Trill spends most of the time listening to my iPod and smiling at our whisper-bickering. At least half an hour goes by with us trekking through the forest, and then suddenly Trill stumbles to a stop. His music becomes frenzied and panicked.

I stop dead a second later when an overpowering polyphony sweeps through the trees, so strong I have to grab hold of a tree to keep my balance. The wind music is so loud it howls like a storm. Trill squeezes my hand, but he doesn't have to say a word.

"Careful with the thorns on these silk cotton trees," Dad warns, examining a tree with spikes—the same kind that curved into my flesh.

I gesture for everyone to be quiet. "Douens, up ahead," I whisper.

We hold hands—me with Trill and Peace, Peace with Mum, and Mum with Dad, and then we slowly enter a tower of trees. The canopy opens up enough for the moon to shed light around the clearing.

The silk cotton trees are humongous, with trunks as big as the meditation space at the facility, and a rash of large, spiky thorns sticks out along their bark like frozen hands. In carved spaces at the base of the trunks are sleeping red douens—way too many to count, curled up like embryos.

A douen's den.

Trill tugs at my hand, trying to advance, but I can't move. Everything about me is too loud for this space—my breathing, my heartbeat. I'm afraid to even blink in case it's too noisy.

I'm going to get my family killed. We have to turn back. I shake my head and take a slow, careful step backward, but Trill refuses to let go of my hand.

He mouths without an echo. *Only way.*

My parents stare at us anxiously, waiting on me to make a decision. Peace gives my hand a small squeeze. They're putting their trust and faith in me.

I can do this. I silently exhale and then give everyone a reassuring nod.

We ease through the trees, taking gentle, tiny footsteps as if we're walking on a balance beam. Peace grips my hand so tightly it brings water to my eyes, but I keep my head down and use the pain to stay focused. I can't afford to start doing a subconscious hum to settle my nerves.

Lift. Step. Pause. Breathe.

Lift. Step. Pause. Breathe.

You don't need any music for this scene. Just quiet heartbeats and steady breathing as we make our way across the space.

And then there's a crack.

A tiny one, but it sounds like a gunshot in the silence. Someone has stepped on a dead branch.

We hold our breaths, and with a clenched jaw, I wait to see if we've stirred the sleeping douens, but there's no movement.

After a few seconds, Trill tugs gently on my hand for us to continue walking.

Lift. Step. Pause. Breathe.

Lift. Step. Pause. Breathe.

Soon the silk cotton trees disappear, giving way again to the thick brush, and though we still don't utter a sound, some of the tightness in my chest eases away.

As we walk, the sky gets lighter and the atmosphere

foggier. I check my watch: fifteen minutes before five a.m., almost sunrise. The soil gives way to tiny pebbles, then to rock, until finally I hear it—the sound of the ocean.

"We made it!" I exclaim, and rush forward, hungry for a glimpse of the sea.

Serenity, Trill booms in the loudest echo I've ever heard.

I come to a stop just in time. If it wasn't for him, I would have burst through the brush and right over the edge of a cliff.

Trill looks up at the sky and then points at an area to the left; it's another cliff edge, but with rocks that look like cracked cannonballs, slanted enough for a steep climb.

"You're not serious," Mum says, and I agree.

"It's hard limestone," Dad says with a frown, examining the rock. "It seems sturdy, but there's been some erosion. We'd need to be careful."

Serenity, Trill says again, but in an urgent tone. *To the beach.*

"I'll go down first and make sure it's okay," Dad says. "Listen out for my signal." Trill does his cowboy whistle, and Dad laughs. "Sure, why not?"

"You'll have to be really loud so we can hear it. Really loud," I say in a cheeky voice that I hope hides my fear. There's nothing anyone can do if he slips and falls into the gray nothingness.

Dad rubs his knuckles on the side of my head and hugs everyone, even Trill. He gives us a corny salute before disappearing down into the fog.

We keep peering over the edge, just in case he decides to return.

"I believe you have something that belongs to me."

I know, I know, I'm tired of villains appearing from behind too.

We whirl around to see a furious Jacob, his gray tunic muddy and torn, and an equally dirty Uncle Newton, who beams at us and waves. I should have heard them coming, but I was too tired and distracted.

"Fancy meeting you here! Will you take a look at this slammin' view," Uncle Newton chirps, putting his hands on his hips and gazing at the gray clouds.

Mum spreads her arms in front of me and Peace to protect us, but Trill steps forward again. This time, no cherries will save the day; Jacob's too far removed from nature.

He is lost. I get it now.

"Oh no you don't."

Jacob reveals a silver butterfly caught between his fingers—the one with the crescent-shaped circles. It tries to flap its wings and silver dust falls onto the ground. The butterfly's music is distressed—it sounds like wind chimes knocking together.

Trill buckles, his face bent with pain. I glance at the

butterfly's crescent patterns, then back at Trill's half-moon birthmark on his cheek, and finally make the connection. It is Trill's butterfly. His soul.

Trill hisses at Jacob like an angry cat.

"That's right, so don't do anything ignorant. Those douens"—Jacob says the word like it's a disease—"destroyed my lab. All my research gone. Hopefully that idiot backed up the data on an external server. I can re-create the chrysalises but I need DNA, so hand over the baby."

"You're too late," I tell him, my eyes focused on the butterfly. "It's gone. And so is Dr. Whisper. Like all evil scientists, he was defeated by his own creation."

Jacob jabs a finger at me. "You're lying."

"I'm not. By the way, cocoon baby is a way cooler name than chrysalis."

"Where's your father?" Jacob demands, looking around. "He must have it." I pray Dad doesn't choose this moment to do the cowboy whistle.

I try to distract him. "This is the point in the movie when the villain—that's you, by the way—realizes they've failed. What are you going to do now, Jacob? Hopefully the smart thing and escape while you can and live to fight another day. Can't you hear them coming?"

I'm not just trying to buy time. The melody of the douens is in the air, probably the same ones from the nearby nest, awoken by the distressed, silent cries of the butterfly.

Jacob narrows his eyes but shifts his gaze to the bush. He removed so much of his soul, he must not be able to hear the douens' music anymore. Trill uses the moment of distraction to rush at Jacob.

Jacob yelps and lets go of the butterfly as Trill tackles him to the ground. It flutters on the ground instead of flying away; its wings must be damaged. I try to save it, but Mum grips my shoulder and hustles Peace and me to the boulders. "Move it."

Jacob and Trill roll around dangerously close to the edge.

"But—"

"MOVE IT!"

And I don't waste another minute. When Naamah Noah yells, she means business. I guide Peace down the rocks, still keeping an eye on the fight. Trill is stronger, but Jacob still has amazing speed and manages to dodge Trill's blow, his fist banging into the rocks. Jacob takes advantage of the moment and pins Trill underneath him.

"Now, now, boys, play nice," Uncle Newton says, wagging his finger.

"Stop them, you dope!" Jacob yells, jerking his chin at us.

Uncle Newton rushes forward and I finally see the semblance to Naamah Noah—the retired road tennis player. Mum takes a running leap and tackles him.

At first, I thought my body was shaking with delight at seeing my prissy mum transform into a live-action superhero, but when Peace cries out and the rocks break away, I realize the cliff is collapsing.

"Mum!" I cry out and reach for Peace, but the ground crumbles underneath us.

A firm grip around my wrist stops my date with death.

Mum has grabbed on to Peace as well. Her face is tight with the effort to hold both our weight, our legs dangling in the air. She tries to pull us back over the ledge, but another piece of rock breaks away and falls into the gray fog.

Mum's grip slips on my sweaty hand and she lets out a panicked cry. I can't believe my story ends on a cliffhanger. Literally.

Peace starts to whimper beside me.

"Mum, just save Peace. It's okay."

"No," Mum says, her voice strained. She tries to pull us both over the ledge again, but my hand slides out of her grip. She catches my wrist and squeezes it even tighter.

"Let me go, Mum," I beg, but she ignores me. Her face starts to turn red and sweat drips from her forehead, and then there's a low chuckle above us.

Jacob appears beside Mum. "And now we get to see *Naamah's Choice*. A tragic family drama, coming to a cinema near you."

"Help me, please," she begs, but he mocks her with his eyes.

"I couldn't have planned this better if I tried," he exclaims with glee.

And in true villain style, Jacob's too busy reveling in victory to notice his own dangerous predicament until it's too late. The rocks weaken under his feet as well.

Jacob's eyes fly open in shock and his hands fight with the air.

"Son!" Uncle Newton yells, his voice laced with terror.

As Jacob is about to topple over the edge, Uncle Newton pushes him out of the way and falls backward into the clouds.

TAKE 37—A CHICKEN

People say their lives flash before their eyes when they're about to die, but that's not how it happened for me.

While I stared at the gray clouds that swallowed Uncle Newton, all I could think about was my future. I want to design more paper monsters with my brother, learn about folklore and history with Dad, persuade Mum to teach me how to play road tennis, and finally . . . see one of my films on the big screen. I'm overwhelmed by how much I want to *live*.

Then strong, rough fingers close around my hand.

Serenity.

And just like that, I can breathe again. I don't have to read Trill's lips to know his meaning: I've got you.

Mum understood it too. Her grip loosens just enough to make sure I'm secure, and then she trusts Trill to drag me over the cliff while she rescues Peace. As soon as we're safe, she gives Peace and me the biggest, warmest hug—one filled with a mother's love. She rains kisses on top of our heads.

Trill cups his butterfly in one hand, crawls over to the edge of the forest, and gently rests the butterfly on the ground. He scoops up a handful of earth and trickles it over the butterfly and his injured hand.

I glance around for Jacob; he's still in the danger area, staring over the edge of the cliff in silence. His score is now a lone wolf howling to the moon. I expect him to erupt in animalistic rage, but when he turns around, there's a perplexed expression on his face.

"He saved me," Jacob says in a tiny voice, staring at us but not seeing us at all. His words are both a question and a statement.

Everyone is silent. Peace takes a step toward Jacob, but I stop him and shake my head. It's not safe. Jacob's music is rife with pain, even though it's not reflected in his face. He could lash out at any second.

"Why did he do that?" Jacob asks, to everyone and no one. A tear rolls down his cheek. He touches the wetness, then looks at his finger in surprise. I'm not sure who's crying— Jacob, Uncle Newton's son, or Elijah, the lost douen who grew to love him as a father.

There's a spark of light behind Jacob. At first, I wonder if the sunrise is breaking through the clouds, but a small silver butterfly appears, so tiny it's hard to see the colors under its wings.

Is that . . . Uncle Newton?

The butterfly flutters down on Jacob's cheek and starts to drink his tears. That's Uncle Newton all right; still trying to comfort him in any form. Jacob stands absolutely still and more tears run down his cheeks, providing a fine feast for Uncle Newton. I can almost hear him saying, "This is groovy!"

It's hard for me to look at his stricken face and not feel some pity.

"Jacob, you don't get it." I take a step closer, but still out of reach. "The perfect family is one that loves you. You may not get along all the time, but they're there for you when it really matters. Uncle Newton was your family so he sacrificed himself for you, without a thought. You were so focused on finding the perfect family, you didn't realize you had it all along."

Jacob lowers his eyes. "I did everything for douenkind. For better lives for them."

"Look around," I reply, gesturing to Trill. He smiles warmly as the healed silver butterfly flutters around his mouth, as if giving him small kisses like Mum did earlier.

"The douens don't need to be 'saved.' They already have a life that's perfect for them."

The silver butterfly flies into the trees. Trill stares after it for a few moments and then approaches Jacob. He takes his hand and pulls him away from the cliff's edge slowly, without disturbing Uncle Newton from quenching his thirst on his face.

Trill mouths to Jacob.

"I don't understand," Jacob says in a frustrated manner. Uncle Newton flutters his wings at his change in expression and Jacob immediately relaxes his face.

"He said, 'Now you can take care of Uncle Newton.'"

There's rustling in the nearby bushes and our gazes follow the sound. I catch my breath, but it's only a rabbit.

Timoteeth!

Though he needs a new name because his humongous curved tooth is gone. The magic of the forest must have restored the rabbits to their natural state as well. There's already a patch of brown fur growing on his head. He rolls around in a pile of leaves and starts to nibble one for breakfast, then his ear perks up.

The douens! Their music is definitely closer. And they're not happy.

"They're coming!" I pull Mum and Peace toward another part of the cliff. This area is steeper and uneven, but at least it's not collapsing.

"No way," she replies, shaking her head. "It's too dangerous."

"But at least we'll have a chance. We're not gonna survive an encounter with a hundred red douens." Trill nods in agreement and hops down the side of the cliff. He tests the rocks for safety.

"Hold on tight." Mum takes my backpack, lightening my load, and also lifts Peace onto her back. "Stay close, Serenity," she says, before following Trill down the cliff.

Serenity.

I turn to see two red douens burst from the bushes, chanting my name. Unlike Trill, there's pure venom in their echo. This time Timoteeth doesn't stick around; he hops into the bushes, leaving his breakfast behind.

Jacob takes Butterfly-Newton off his cheek with a finger and cups him in his hands to protect him. But there's nowhere to run; the douens have us cornered.

I think about climbing down the cliff, but that's dangerous enough without douens on my tail. They know this land better than I do and I'd be putting myself in a more vulnerable position. And worse, it'll endanger my family as well; Mum and Peace need more time to reach the bottom.

The red douens point their fingers at us, ones with sharp, jagged nails, and whisper my name again. Now I understand this is the move right before they attack, like when a snake flattens its head just before it's about to strike.

I only have one idea to buy my family more time.

I take a deep breath and scream.

But not just any scream. I roar *a chicken* over and over again, remembering all those times I wanted to shout it at the top of my lungs.

The douens squat and cover their ears, mouths twisted in agony and anger. One of them takes a step closer but then buckles again.

Jacob joins in, but he's no match for my inner Jackie Opel.

I channel the singer's energy, thinking about how he entertained those guests at the top of the cruise ship from the ocean.

My throat is on fire but I don't stop bellowing, not until the douens decide to give up and jump into the bushes.

I keep chanting as I start to climb down the edge, though I can feel my vocal cords trembling from the effort. The last thing I see before I move out of sight is Jacob's sad smile.

Even after all his deceit, I don't want him to die. He's a hurt, broken person, so maybe the magic of the forest can heal him too. But right now, I have my own family to worry about.

If I had to score this scene, I'd compose something that sounds like poetic justice.

TAKE 38—SHELVED

I usually walk past a sea view without looking up from my phone.

Never again.

I've never felt such joy as when I get the first glimpse of the darkish-blue water. There's a peek of orange in the lightening sky, but it's still dark enough for the bush along the beach to look like crowded shadows. The water is eerily still, but best to use the sound of gentle waves for dramatic effect.

I meet Trill near the bottom of the cliff. He was climbing back up to get me. He guides me down the last few rocks, where Dad, Mum, and Peace are waiting on the sand.

My parents wrap me in an embrace, concerned about my screaming, but I just point at my throat and gesture that I'm okay.

Right now it hurts to talk, but I'm also choked up with emotion.

I can't believe we made it. We've been through so much, the natural and supernatural, yet here we are, together.

But the thrill of our reunion doesn't last long. Peace tugs at my shirt and points up at the trees. A group of silver butterflies nestles down on some branches, as if preparing to watch a show.

"Get to the jetty!" Dad shouts, and we all dash toward it, hoping to see the Captain's ferry in the distance.

Almost all of us. Something is missing. I turn to see Trill still at the edge of the forest.

Not a "something," but a "someone." Then the reality of the situation hits me—he can't come with us.

I run toward him and he comes forward a few steps to meet me.

I'm so sorry, I mouth.

"Serenity . . ." Mum calls.

I gasp when Dad grabs me by the waist, lifts me off my feet, and charges toward the jetty.

"Wait!" I say in a raspy voice. I struggle away from Dad and then grab my backpack from Mum. I remove a charger and race back to the trees, ignoring my parents' cries.

At this point in the movie, some folks may be shouting at their screens, claiming we don't have time for this last emotional moment. They would be right.

The red douens are coming and they'll rip us apart, but I need to say goodbye. Who knows if I'll ever see Trill again? With the clinic gone, there's no safe place for humans on Duppy Island.

Trill meets me halfway, and his face becomes wrinkled and gray before my eyes. I give him a quick hug and then shove the iPod charger in his hands. Douens are intelligent; he'll find a way to make it work so he can listen to spouge beats for years to come.

From the end of the jetty, we watch as Trill's skin tightens back into a matte brown—moments after, he's in the shadows of the forest.

"I won't let anyone forget you!" Dad shouts.

Trill mimics Dad's corny salute before jumping into the bushes.

Now everyone can hear the whispers in the trees.

"Don't panic," Dad says in a high-pitched, squeaky voice. He's clearly talking to himself.

I check my watch. It'll be sunrise in about half an hour. Much too long away.

"The douens won't be able to reach us out here. You saw what happened to Trill," Mum says, casting a longing look at the trees.

I'm not convinced. The red douens are much older than Trill and may have more endurance. Plus Jacob made it all the way to the mainland.

Then dozens of short bodies and mushroom hats appear on the beach.

Hurt. Hurt. Hurt.

We bunch together with bated breaths, but then our worst

fears come true when one of the taller red douens starts to creep toward the jetty and the others begin to follow.

"Scream," I say hoarsely.

Mum and Dad try their best, but their combined cries only annoy the douens, like mosquitoes buzzing in their ears. Though Peace's scream causes a few creatures to flinch, there's no way he can hold them off by himself.

I grab the crank radio from the backpack and turn the flashlight on full blast. The glare is enough to send a few douens at the front reeling back. But then the light starts to flicker.

"The battery is dying!" Mum exclaims.

Dad grabs the radio and frantically cranks it to bring charge, but the light is weak and the douens begin to advance again.

"We're gonna have to swim for it," Dad yells, giving up on the radio.

I shake my head frantically. "Jellyfish," I say, but it comes out as a broken squeak.

But then I remember something else. After muttering a short prayer, I grab the crank radio from Dad and throw it as far as I can into the ocean.

"What are you doing?!" Mum cries.

At first, nothing happens. Then a glowing white light appears in the water. Then a blue one. And pink and orange. It looks like pulsing disco lights, coming on one at a time.

The now-disturbed jellyfish illuminate the sea along the jetty and the edge of the water. The Captain was true to his words: It's like the aurora borealis at night.

The douens shield their faces and back away from the jetty, and their hisses of frustration fill the air. They jump into the bushes to get away from the glowing light.

We sit on the jetty, huddled as close together as we can, gazing at our umbrella-shaped saviors in the water. They're like translucent lily pads floating in the sea, only with beautiful and deadly ribbon tentacles.

"You know," Dad says, breaking the silence, "jellyfish are seen to be symbols for survival. Though the odds are stacked against them, they are guided by instinct. They don't fight the current, but move with the flow and blend into the environment. I think people can learn a lot from them."

No one replies, but Mum rests her head on his shoulder, and their pitter-patter music calms my mind enough for me to fall asleep. I wake up as the sun rises, the sky going to light gray with an orange kiss, and see the Captain's ferry in the horizon.

We survived, just like the jellyfish.

I look at the beach, where there are several backward footprints in the sand. There's no way to make out which ones belong to Trill.

I don't even have a picture of him.

The thought makes me wonder about the footage on the

camera. It may have captured Dr. Whisper's full confession about his terrible experiments with douens and kids in the Your Perfect Child program. I can imagine producers would be interested in making a full TV series about this adventure, not just a movie. If I exposed him, I'd be interviewed on national TV, invited to talk shows, blow up on social media and—

Then I realize what all this attention would mean for Trill. If the world gets proof of douens, Duppy Island will be flooded with unwelcome visitors. Other scientists or government officials may turn Trill and the other douens into lab rats, or worse. Suppose they put them in a circus?

Dr. Whisper mentioned he had nine other "successes." That's nine other kids who have been replaced with douens, including Eloise. If they're exposed in an investigation, the kids could be taken away from their families. The douen-human children are victims too; they have no memories of their previous selves. I lost my parents for one day and it rocked me to my core—I couldn't live with myself if I caused that pain for someone else.

I say a sad, silent goodbye to my five minutes of fame. When my camera is recharged, I have to delete the footage from the clinic. This movie will never be made.

No one will ever get a chance to direct this film.

Minutes later, when the ferry docks on the jetty, the Captain doesn't ask us any questions. He and Horace unload crates onto the jetty as normal, with my parents helping so we can get off the island as soon as possible.

"Do you hear that guitar?" Peace asks me.

I shake my head. "What does it sound like?"

Peace ponders before he gives an answer. "I can't describe it, but it makes me feel warm inside."

Before I can reply, a whistle comes from the trees. A cowboy whistle. Trill's final goodbye.

Horace twists his head around. "What's that?"

"I heard nothing," says the Captain, and starts the motor. Horace shrugs and goes to lift the anchor. Peace hums Horace's clinking fish hook music under his breath and giggles.

I gape at him and am struck again by the image of Jacob lifting the syringe above me. Did he do more than erase my memories when he caught me in the lab six years ago? I put the thought out of my head forever. That's a question I don't want the answer to.

In my heart, I say goodbye to Duppy Island and smile at the thought of my great-great-great-great-great-great-uncle, a legendary musician, dancing to spouge beats in his safe place.

THAT'S A WRAP

It's up to you to decide what really happened on Duppy Island.

Maybe I'm just a bored twelve-year-old storyteller with a lot of time and imagination. You *could* believe that we just went on a camping trip and managed to capture footage of an endangered butterfly. That's what my dad told the authorities. He recommended that further developments on the island be restricted. No one should travel there.

If you were thinking about making a movie, consider a documentary about the forgotten deaths of the victims of the cholera pandemic sent to Duppy Island in 1854—wait, sorry, that idea is already taken. The Noah family came together to produce it, and with Dad's scriptwriting, Peace's production design, Mum's hair and makeup, and my directing and scoring skills, it's sure to be a hit at the film festival next summer.

Dad wants to name the film *The Forgotten Ones on Duppy Island*. I want to call it *When the Land Became Sick—The*

Tragic Tale of the Abandoned. Everyone but Peace thinks my title is too dramatic. We'll find the perfect name, I'm sure, but it's okay if we don't.

Sometimes good enough is perfect.

Peace and I still intend to make the scariest horror movie of all time. I haven't decided on the plot yet, but all the characters will wear blank masks and the audience will have to determine the heroes and the monsters by their actions.

Oh, and the main character will be called Trill. No special reason.

I just like the sound of the name.

ACKNOWLEDGMENTS

If I could hear the scores of all the people involved in making this book, what would they sound like?

They would start with the sound of approval from my agent, Marietta Zacker, who confirmed that a story about a family stuck on an island of douens was cool and creepy. I think her score would be quiet cheers interspersed with clapping.

My brainstorming gurus—Lisa, Alexia, Gina, and Sharma—would sound like the constant flickering of lightbulbs while they helped me with a plethora of ideas for Serenity's character and plot. I would not have been able to build this world without their light.

It's not possible for one score to fit my editor, Mallory Kass. I think her music would be an entire musical arrangement, starting with the tap of the conductor's baton. Cue the gentle harp strings of encouragement sprinkled with fairy dust as she worked her editorial magic on my manuscript. Then the swish of the baton, guiding the brilliance of Scholastic's editorial, production, and marketing teams. I am still wowed by the talent of illustrator Godwin Akpan and cover designer Omou Barry. Thank you to David Levithan, Jalen Garcia-Hall, Emily Heddleson, Janell Harris, Elizabeth

Parisi, Alan Smagler, Jarad Waxman, Rachel Feld, Elisabeth Ferrari, Katie Dutton, and Lizette Serrano. I am always grateful for the opportunity to sit in the audience and be wowed by Scholastic's orchestra.

My friend Liesl is the fun, clinking sound that brings joy—the kind of tune you would listen to when you need motivation. She's the knock on the door with "you got this" cupcakes (thank you, Michelle and Sky!).

Malissa is the cat's purr that brings peace in the midst of chaos. And just like a cat, she has the innate ability to show up with affection when you need it the most.

Lloyda is the comforting pitter-patter of raindrops that makes you want to curl up in bed. She can also turn into a rainstorm if anyone dares to cause me harm.

Together, Danielle and Deirdre are the nostalgic beat from your favorite song that always makes you smile—the one you hum when you need to relax.

A clink of glasses in a toast of appreciation to Sandra, Akeeba, Stefan, Ryan, Nicole, Chrystal, Daka, Gail, Allison, Ellen, Dana, Roger, Ayesha, Ramona, and Shelly.

Thank you to all my readers, who must sound like turning pages, allowing me to continue to write these stories.

Here's where I thank everyone I forgot to mention by name. I know your soundtracks may echo impatient, tapping fingers, but I plan to write many more books so you will make it into one of these acknowledgments eventually.

My husband, Gibbs, is the music that's hard to describe—
the one that would feel like a warm hug and a bellyful of
laughter. Thank you for being my rhythm of happiness.

As you know, I can't hear my own score, but I hope I'd
sound like a tapping keyboard, writing the next story.

ABOUT THE AUTHOR

Shakirah Bourne is a Bajan author and filmmaker born and based in Barbados. She once shot a movie scene in a cave with bats during an earthquake, but is too scared to watch horror movies. She enjoys exploring old graveyards, daydreaming, and eating mangoes. Learn more at shakirahbourne.com.